RIVERDALE

THE POISON PEN

RIVERDALE

THE POISON PEN

An original novel by Caleb Roehrig

SCHOLASTIC INC.

Copyright © 2020 by Archie Comic Publications, Inc.

All rights reserved. Published by Scholastic Inc., *Publishers since 1920*. SCHOLASTIC and associated logos are trademarks and/or registered trademarks of Scholastic Inc.

The publisher does not have any control over and does not assume any responsibility for author or third-party websites or their content.

No part of this publication may be reproduced, stored in a retrieval system, or transmitted in any form or by any means, electronic, mechanical, photocopying, recording, or otherwise, without written permission of the publisher. For information regarding permission, write to Scholastic Inc., Attention: Permissions Department, 557 Broadway, New York, NY 10012.

This book is a work of fiction. Names, characters, places, and incidents are either the product of the author's imagination or are used fictitiously, and any resemblance to actual persons, living or dead, business establishments, events, or locales is entirely coincidental.

ISBN 978-1-338-66967-1

1 2020

Printed in the U.S.A.   23

First printing 2020

Book design by Jessica Meltzer

Secrets are like cockroaches: When you spot one, you know there are hundreds more just below the surface. And the town of Riverdale is infested. I would know.

I've learned a lot just by observing the people here. For example, when Archie and Betty were pretending to hook up as part of their ruse to smoke out Jughead's would-be murderers? It was pretty clear to me that their little "spring fling" wasn't a total sham. The way they'd sneak glances at each other when they thought no one was watching... all you had to do was catch the expressions on their faces, and you could read their true feelings like the menu at Pop's.

I don't mean to brag, but I figured out Veronica had something going on with Reggie while her erstwhile boyfriend was busy rotting away in juvie for murder. And Kevin Keller was so obvious about his fling with Moose Mason, back when it was still supposed to be hush-hush, that he might as well have just taken out a full-page ad in the Register to announce that they were sneaking around on the sly.

Some people might call me nosy. (And I guess there's a little truth to that, even if I don't really think of it that way myself.) The simple fact is, in a town like Riverdale? You have to try <u>hard</u> to avoid stumbling over other people's private business. None of us went looking for news about Hiram and Hermione Lodge's collapsing marriage, none of us really wanted updates on Betty Cooper's creepy <u>Silence of the Lambs</u> relationship with her father, and we didn't ask Cheryl Blossom to give us all a minute-by-minute update of her romance with Toni Topaz. But we got all of it, anyway, just the same.

How can a person be considered nosy when the secrets in this town practically go looking for <u>us</u>, rather than the other way around? Honestly, minding your own business is a full-time job in Riverdale. And I've got too much to do as it is.

Recently, I learned something particularly juicy—something I was definitely not supposed to know. I spotted one of those pesky little cockroaches, and before I could even think twice, I was flipping over the proverbial rock and finding dozens more. To tell you the truth, it made me sick.

And then it made me mad.

Maybe Riverdale has never been the perfect little greeting-card town people like to pretend it is, but I'm sick of wading knee-deep in metaphorical cockroaches.

So I guess you could say I've appointed myself

our little hamlet's own personal exterminator. Too many beautiful people are keeping too many ugly things hidden, and I'm done being a silent witness to it all. So grab your sunglasses, kids, because I'm shining a great big light into this town's dark corners, and what comes out might shock you . . .

—Poison Pen

PART ONE
VERONICA LODGE
SATURDAY

Senator and Mrs.
Patrick Pendergast

request the pleasure of your company at
a cocktail reception to celebrate
the engagement of their daughter

Pernilla Phoebe

to

Deputy Hayes Huxley

On Saturday the eighth of August
at eight o'clock in the evening

Five Seasons Hotel Ballroom
57230 Evelyn Street
Riverdale

*The favor of a reply
is requested.*

RSVP to: Veronica Lodge and Cheryl Blossom

CHAPTER ONE

Summers in Riverdale can be positively beastly—sticky as maple syrup, and not nearly as sweet. Lucky for me, the Five Seasons Hotel has particularly robust central air, and the suite that housed the Maple Club was as crisp as an October afternoon. I was also fortunate that the Maple Girls were willing to put in diligent labor right up to the last minute to prepare for that evening's event. The room bustled with activity as we all bundled party favors, hand-lettered place cards, and decorated personalized flasks of rum.

"I have to hand it to you, Veronica," Cheryl Blossom said graciously, tossing her red hair over her shoulder as she admired the embossed cream-and-silver card stock of the invitations I'd designed. "With only three weeks to plan it, you've managed to put together an event that looks like you had . . . well, let's say at least four weeks."

"Thank you so much." My tone was dry—but the fact is, this backhanded praise was about as undiluted as compliments got when they came from Cheryl Blossom. "Flattery will get you nowhere."

"Don't listen to her." This was Toni Topaz, Cheryl's girlfriend. Her pink hair held back by a patterned headband, she was carefully filling out a sheet of blank labels with a calligraphy pen. "In three weeks, you wrangled together ice sculptures, celebrity guests, a chef flown in from actual France to prepare the hors d'oeuvres, got a mixologist from the 21 Club to design an original cocktail named after the bride-to-be . . . *and* you're using it as an opportunity to promote Red Raven Rum? Not many people could pull this off."

"Thank you," I repeated, a bit more sincerely. This was the kind of appreciation I deserved for all the headaches I'd suffered over the past month. And I'd suffered plenty.

"Even if the marriage *is* totally doomed, and we all know it is, and I feel like some kind of vulture filling out these labels right now," she added under her breath.

And there it was. I let out a defeated sigh and sank deeper into my seat, banging the keys of my laptop a little more aggressively, scrolling once more through a slideshow presentation that would be one of the evening's pivotal moments. Wishing I could disappear into my computer for good.

"Listen, ladies, we've been over this"—*and over this, and over this*—"so let's just drop it, okay?"

Cheryl reached out and gave her girlfriend's hand an affectionate squeeze. "All TeeTee means, Veronica, is that because this young couple is heading for the kind of dramatic crash and burn you see in Michael Bay disaster movies, capitalizing on their engagement feels a little bit . . . crass. That's all."

"Thank you for interpreting, Cheryl, but I picked up on that." Letting out a louder and more exasperated sigh, I gave up on the slideshow and massaged my temples. "Look. When Pernilla approached me about hosting her engagement party, I didn't ask questions before saying yes. The Pendergasts are a political dynasty, and I knew the guest list—*this* guest list," I noted emphatically, scooping up the roster of names from a pile beside me, "would be a who's who of influencers and tastemakers around the world. I didn't know the details until I'd already made a commitment. And by that time, I couldn't exactly back out without an explanation, could I?"

I fixed the both of them with a meaningful glare. They understood me. We all knew the Pendergast-Huxley marriage was doomed, and why, even if we could never say so aloud. It was knowledge we weren't supposed to have, for one thing, and those of us involved had even gone so far as to swear an oath never to speak of it again. For many reasons, I had no intention of violating our pact—but especially not with sensitive ears present. Glancing up, I caught Penelope Blossom watching me from a corner of the room, as if she could read my thoughts, and I shivered. We had wanted her where we could keep her in our sights, but her constant presence in the club was unnerving.

I *could* still call the event off, of course, with no explanation at all—but it would bring ruination down on our names, and we'd worked too hard for that. I had volunteered to provide a hundred and fifty personalized flasks of Red Raven Rum, labeled and numbered by hand, as favors for all the guests of our grand soiree. No matter what disasters befell the couple of the evening, Cheryl and I would emerge from the debacle a great success as both event planners and mavens of the social scene. I would accept no other outcome.

Senator Pendergast, of course, had his own outcomes in mind. Hayes Huxley was a local—the same age as Polly Cooper—and he was a deputy with the Rockland County Sheriff's Office to boot. The senator's daughter saying yes to a small-town cop only a few months before the upcoming gubernatorial elections was the kind of publicity and outreach money couldn't buy.

And Patrick Pendergast had *scads* of money.

"Well. At least when their marriage collapses, it won't be our fault," Cheryl said cheerfully, reaching for a box of crystal champagne flutes etched with the engaged couple's initials. Each was to have a length of silver ribbon wound around its delicate stem.

No one, and I mean *no one*, would ever say that I throw an understated party.

There came a knock at the door of the suite, and I dispatched Laura—one of the Maple Girls—to answer it, turning back to the presentation I was reviewing on my laptop. After the speeches, but before the dancing started, I was going to introduce a slideshow celebrating the relationship of the soon-to-be-wed couple. I'd worked with the family to select the perfect photographs, I'd worked with a professional editor to make sure the transitions were seamless and artful, and I'd even managed to convince Josie McCoy to record a song for the accompaniment. It was going to be flawless, I was certain . . . but it didn't hurt to double-check. Or triple-check, as the case may be.

When Laura returned to the room, she held a plain white envelope in her hand. "It was just a guy bringing up the mail. I guess someone left this for you at the front desk, Veronica."

It's funny how your life can change irrevocably, but the moment it happens is so mundane you never see it coming. Everyone fears the big catastrophes—your boyfriend's father dying in a tragic accident, for example, or your own father developing an unpredictable illness. When you've lived through all that, who's afraid of an envelope?

In retrospect, I'm embarrassed to admit that I wasn't.

It was a perfect square, my name printed across the front in meticulous block lettering. There was no return address on the missive—although I guess there wouldn't be, if someone had left it at the front desk—and the flap was sealed with a coin of scarlet wax. It was a charming touch, old-fashioned and debonair, and I smiled. The insignia pressed into the shiny red disc was a curlicue *PP*.

Assuming it was from one of the Pendergasts—some final instructions, or maybe (what a laugh) even a *thank-you* for all our hard work—I opened it without hesitation.

Dear Ronniekins,

I know you've got your hands full, making all the arrangements for Pernilla Pendergast's fabulous engagement party, so I'll be brief. (Wait! Being Veronica Lodge, no doubt you prefer a word that's far more pretentious and grandiose than party to describe a gaggle of wealthy drunkards coming together to congratulate one another on their acquaintanceship. Let me guess . . . fete? Soiree? Stop me if I get it!)

You love to play the part of the poor little rich girl, don't you? All that false humility, all that disclaiming of your father . . . except when his wrongdoings work in your favor. Veronica Lodge: Mafia Princess with a Heart of Gold.

What a crock.

How many of Daddy's crimes have you been complicit in, or silent about? How many people has he hurt, how many lives has he destroyed, while you looked the other way through your Cartier sunglasses?

How many crimes have you committed yourself? I know of at least one. On the night of July Fourth, while most of Riverdale was passing around snacks and sodas at the fireworks display in Pickens Park, you filed a false police report and defrauded your insurance company. Daddykins would be so proud. You're a real chip off the old cell block.

Now, I know what you're thinking: Those transgressions are small potatoes compared to what else goes on in this town. Your name alone has gotten you out of worse trouble than what you'd face if somebody tattled on you to the sheriff. But here's what you should keep in mind: I know <u>everything</u> that happened that night. What you did. Why you did it. Who else was involved.

And, Ronnie? I have proof.

So start thinking about what it's worth to you to keep this little secret hushed up, because soon, there's a favor I'm going to need from you. Meanwhile, be a lamb and keep this note a secret? Don't tell anyone—not Daddy and not a single one of your friends—or I'll know, and there <u>will</u> be consequences. I'm watching you . . .

—Poison Pen

CHAPTER TWO

I froze, my heart dropping through the floor. Tucked into the fold of the note was a photograph. Of me. I had a coffee in one hand, a stack of blank labels in the other, and a smile on my face. It had been taken in the lobby of the Five Seasons not three hours earlier, when I'd arrived for the day.

I gripped the edge of the table to steady myself. Perhaps I made some sort of noise—a gasp or a squeak—because when I looked up, the entire room had eyes on me.

"Veronica?" Cheryl straightened, clearly worried. "Is everything all right? You look like my nana Rose when Mumsie would withhold her blood pressure medication."

For a beat too long, I stared at her, trying to marshal my out-of-control thoughts. Twisting my mouth into something that I hoped looked like a smile, I forced out, "I'm fine. I'm just . . . hungry. That's all."

"Are you sure?" Cheryl's eyes narrowed, and I felt like I was laid flat on an X-ray table, her fixed gaze reading right through me. "Because I know what 'hungry' looks like. Mumsie was also a fan of withholding food to coerce good behavior."

From her corner, Penelope gave a loud snort in response—which could have been a scoff or a smug burst of laughter—and the three of us glared at her in unison.

"I'm *fine*," I repeated, a bit more firmly, squeezing my hands into fists to keep them from visibly shaking.

Toni, of course, also refused to let it go. "What did that letter say?"

For a split second, maybe less, I almost considered telling them the truth. The odious and threatening contents of the note from "Poison Pen" concerned them, too, after all; but I came to my senses in the nick of time.

"Nothing!" I grabbed the offending sheet of paper, stuffing it and the photograph back into their envelope. Then I crammed it all into my purse, snapping the clasp shut like the lid on Pandora's box. "It was . . . from the musicians! Their song list for this evening. It looks fabulous—lots of Haydn and Brahms."

My pitch was all over the place. I sounded utterly unhinged and undeniably guilty, and Cheryl narrowed her eyes even further. "I thought you wanted them to play Vivaldi."

"Plans change!" I was halfway to the door before I knew I was moving, that phony smile beginning to hurt my face. Sipping from a porcelain teacup, Penelope Blossom watched me every step of the way, a chilly little twist teasing up one corner of her mouth. "Anyway, I really am famished, so I'll just pop out and grab some lunch. We've been so busy, I've barely remembered to eat today! Hold down the fort, ladies?"

The door to the suite slammed shut behind me, leaving me all alone in the posh, plush comfort of the hallway—thick carpets, crown molding, raw silk wallpaper—but it spun around me in a blur. My chest heaved, my heart throbbed in my temples, and I sagged against the doorframe, sinking slowly to the floor.

∧∧∧

July Fourth. Independence Day. In our history class last year, we learned that it was the date of Radio Free Europe's first broadcast, in 1950. More recently, it had been the day of Fred Andrews's memorial parade through Riverdale. A few years before that, it had also been the worst day of my life.

Up to that point, anyway.

It was the anniversary of Daddy's arrest. (Well, the first one.) That day had been so unbearably dreadful, and I have to admit that every time the calendar rolled back around to July, my stomach went a little cold. I'd never thought of myself as being inordinately superstitious—I wasn't afraid of black cats, anyway—but every summer since that terrible one back in Manhattan, it was a date I associated with bad luck.

This particular summer, I spent July Fourth in a state of nervous jitters. It was oppressively hot, my schedule crowded by petty demands from my parents and multiple errands I had to run with regard to my various business interests in Riverdale.

My driver had been up since dawn, and by the time we made it to the Five Seasons that evening, it was just after dark and he was positively knackered. "I'll have to stay and put out fires at the Maple Club for another few hours," I told him regretfully, "but I'll book a room for you—on me—so you can at least lie down for a while."

He protested, as decorum required, but I wouldn't take no for an answer. We went into the hotel and to our respective suites, and I promised to wake him when I was ready to leave.

It was, however, only an hour later that I was back in the parking garage, alone . . . and making a hysterical call to the police. I was sobbing, barely able to form intelligible words, but I managed to say that I believed my life was in danger—and that my last name was Lodge—and two deputies were dispatched immediately.

When they arrived, I was cowering in a stairwell in the parking garage, shaking all over, my face streaked with tears. Fifty feet away sat my car. Or what was left of it.

The windows and headlights were completely shattered, the side mirrors dangling like lop ears, and all four tires were flat—slashed. The doors and quarter panels were dented, and the hood . . . a hideous, grinning skull had been spray-painted on the hood of my gorgeous Rolls-Royce in indelible crimson.

I was in such a state that it took the uniformed men some five minutes to calm me down enough to explain. "I w-was working . . . for almost an hour . . . before I realized I'd left my purse in the car—"

"It took you an hour to realize you didn't have your purse?"

"Women care about things other than handbags, *Deputy*," I snarled, glaring daggers at him until he mumbled an apology. "I walked all the way back here—in the dark! Without giving it a second thought! And when I reached the car, I saw . . . I saw . . ." I buried my face in my hands and began to sob again.

"It's all right, miss." The first deputy patted my shoulder the way you might check to see if paint is dry or not. "You're okay. Everything's going to be fine—"

"It is *NOT*!" I practically screeched, my voice echoing up and down the concrete ramps of the parking garage. Summoning my inner Cheryl Blossom, I raged, "Are you on Fizzle Rocks, you Dogpatch backwater halfwit? Look at my car!" With a savage gesture, I indicated the ruined windscreen, the tires, that freakish skull. "What part of this looks all right to you?"

"Believe it or not, it could've been worse. It could have been your head that got smashed in." His reply was curt and intentionally provocative, and his partner intervened.

"What Deputy Carlson means, miss, is that you're safe." He took me by the elbow, angling me away from the sight of both the wrecked car and his disgruntled colleague. "This was probably nothing more than a case of routine vandalism. Is your vehicle insured?"

"Of course it's insured," I answered, beginning to sob yet again, "but that isn't the point! Can't you see that this is personal? That . . . that skull is a threat!"

This, he finally treated seriously. "Are you certain of that, Miss

Lodge? Do you have reason to believe someone wishes to hurt you?"

"Do you know who my father is?" I shot back. "He's made tons of enemies over the years, and plenty of them would hurt me to get back at him!"

Judiciously, I left out the fact that, following his arrest—the second one, I mean, the one I'd set him up for—*I* had occasionally been one of Daddy's enemies.

"I hear what you're saying." He relaxed, visibly, giving me a polite, understanding nod. "But, you know, July Fourth is sort of like a second Devil's Night here in Riverdale. With half the town in Pickens Park for the big show, it's pretty much all hands on deck for law enforcement. A lot of kids are going to get up to mischief tonight, knowing we can't be everywhere at once."

"How can you call this mischief?" I demanded, my voice quavering. "What if my life is in danger? What if this person is waiting for me to leave the garage, and, and—"

In the face of a fresh onslaught of tears, the man held up his hands. "Please, Miss Lodge, don't worry about that right now, okay? We won't leave until we're confident you're safe. Besides, this garage must have security cameras. We can probably clear this up by tomorrow morning."

With a pitiful moan, I flung my hand out yet again. "It's supposed to, but look!"

Bolted to a crossbeam twenty yards away was the metal arm of a camera mount, and on the concrete floor beneath it, beaten and crushed like an old tin can, lay the camera itself.

The deputies made a diligent search of the premises, and when no lurking miscreants were found, they graciously escorted me back to the Five Seasons. I wouldn't let them leave my side until I was letting myself back into the Maple Club, where a slab of solid oak with a dead-bolt lock and a brass door guard stood between me and that long, empty hallway.

"I'm probably going to have to spend the night here," I babbled, not wanting to let the deputies go. "I can't even imagine leaving before the sun comes up. Who knows who might be out there?"

"I'm sure you'll be all right, miss," the senior deputy assured me yet again. "It was probably just a couple of kids blowing off steam. They saw a fancy car, and they got excited." Tipping his hat to me, he began, "We'll leave you to y——"

"Would you two gentlemen care to come inside?" I interrupted, giving them my most charming smile. "I could pour you a drink? You haven't lived until you've tried my maple rum!"

"No, thank you." He shuffled his feet. "We can't drink on duty."

"Really? Not even a little one?" I asked. "I'd like to express my gratitude, and to apologize if I was rude earlier. I . . . I'm not myself tonight. I'm sure you understand."

He opened his mouth to reply—and his radio squawked, an emergency call splitting the thick silence of the Five Seasons hallway. Both men snapped to attention. "I'm sorry, Miss Lodge, but we have to go. Stay inside, and keep the door locked; you'll be all right."

"Thank you, deputies!" I called after them as they sprinted away down the corridor, vanishing into the stairwell.

My entire body slumped the second they were out of sight, all my adrenaline slipping away like water down the drain. I barricaded myself inside the Maple Club, paranoia settling in like an old friend, and I poured myself a healthy dram of rum to steady my nerves. Pulling out my phone, I sent a quick text:

Show's over. House lights up, the audience has gone home.

∿∿∿

The show wasn't as over as I'd thought. But who had my covert spectator been? Who had seen what *really* happened in that garage?

A clatter from around the bend in the corridor announced the approach of a room service cart, and I struggled back to my feet, drawing on all the poise that Daddykins said made me a perfect Lodge. *"Never let them see you sweat,* m'hija. *If you must indulge your weakness, do it in private."* So, when the bellboy rounded the turn, I managed a placid smile and strode for the elevator bank.

I won't pretend I didn't consider doing an about-face and sprinting right back into the Maple Club's suite. If what Poison Pen said was true—*"I know* everything *that happened that night"*—then Cheryl and Toni had a right to know. After all, the secrets I was keeping weren't mine alone. In point of fact, the worst of them weren't even mine at all.

"What you did. Why you did it. Who else is involved."

But if that part of the menacing message could be believed, then what of the rest? *"Don't tell anyone . . . I'll know . . . I'm watching you."* It was preposterously Gothic, like something out of Henry James . . . but could I afford to ignore it? That little photograph of me, entering the Five Seasons with my coffee, made me second-guess all my choices.

I told myself it meant nothing. So what if someone was waiting in the lobby to take that actually rather flattering picture? (My Prada basket clutch was definitely a wise investment, and went perfectly with my aubergine Chloé miniskirt.) It didn't prove that they were actually watching me—and certainly not all the time. No doubt I could speak freely with Cheryl in the ensured privacy of the suite.

Only, there *was* no privacy in the Maple Club at the moment. Until the Pendergasts' little soiree was over and done (*party*—the Pendergasts' *party*), our private space would be at capacity with everyone I'd coaxed, cajoled, and bullied into helping out.

And, if I may be candid, Cheryl's advice wasn't always what you might call sound. If what I wanted was smart, levelheaded guidance, I wasn't going to get it from a girl who once threatened to push Reggie Mantle down the stairs for wearing white after Labor Day. When the elevator arrived, I was already composing a text.

∧∧∧

Veronica:

I know you're busy today, but I really need my ride-or-die right now. Lunch? On me, of course.

Betty:

An offer I can't refuse! Back-to-school shopping with my mother makes me want to go back to the Sisters of Quiet Mercy 💀

Veronica:

Meet me at the library in twenty?

Betty:

Do they . . . serve food at the library now?

Veronica:

No, but they serve privacy. And, trust me, B . . . when you hear what I have to say, you'll be grateful for the isolation. We can go to Pop's after.

Betty:

Okay, V, now you've got me intrigued. And concerned?

Veronica:

All will be explained, B, I promise.

CHAPTER THREE

A friend in need is a friend indeed, and I couldn't ask for a better one than my BFF, Betty Cooper. Life in Manhattan had certainly been blessed, but my family's infamous reversal of fortune had revealed all the snakes slithering in our always-greener grass. At the time, moving to Riverdale had seemed a fate worse than death—exile to a town I couldn't find on the map, where I'd have to live down two reputations at once: spoiled socialite and daughter of a disgraced criminal.

But despite the humiliating slings and arrows, I would go through it all again just to know Betty.

Okay, maybe not the serial killer parts, or that whole saga where my father had a man killed and tried to pin it on my boyfriend, but . . . you know, other stuff.

I was the first to arrive at the library, its clapboard exterior recently whitewashed, its flower garden a jungle of verdant leaves. No matter how unflappable Daddy liked me to be in front of guests and Feds and live cameras, the short jaunt from the Five Seasons had left me entirely *flapped*. It wasn't that I'd caught someone following me; it was that I'd caught *everyone* following me.

It was absurd, a paranoid delusion—and, worse, I knew it—but I couldn't shake the sense that I was being watched. The night of July Fourth lit up in my memory, a fiery sparkler tracing my guilt through the air. The tomblike silence of the parking garage, the carpet of shattered glass . . . two deputies making a thorough search of the stairwells, the shadowy corners, turning up nothing. There had been no one there; and yet someone knew.

Didn't they?

"If you lured me here just to give you book recommendations I could've texted, I'm going to be slightly annoyed." A voice at my shoulder made me jump, and I spun around to see Betty standing behind me. "But only slightly. My mom is being *extremely* OG Alice Cooper today."

She looked . . . well, she looked like *herself.* Contained and color coordinated, dressed in pastels, her blond locks pinned up into her signature ponytail. She was the veritable antithesis of trouble, and I threw my arms around her in a relieved embrace.

"Wow! Not that I mind the PDA, V, but what's going on? You look like you've seen a ghost. Possibly one murdering another ghost."

"I'm just . . . glad you're here," I mumbled, blinking back tears.

"I mean, me too." Betty smiled, tossing a glance in the direction from which she'd come. "My mom just bought five sets of sheets for me, returned three of them, bought two more, and then returned one of *those*. And, believe it or not, she's mad at *me* for not taking sheets more seriously. You gave me an excuse to escape." It was clear she was trying to gauge my mood—and that she was realizing how dark it truly was. "V . . . why did you ask me to meet you here?"

"Inside," I answered, my voice suddenly shaking. The sidewalks were crowded, all the faces too familiar. (My mother had actually once assured me that the intimacy of small-town life would be comforting. *"Everybody knows everybody in Riverdale, m'hija, and they all look out for their own."*) But now I was trapped in a fishbowl, and everyone around me was a hungry cat. It almost made me miss life in Manhattan, where friendly strangers were the ones who wanted to kill you.

I pushed poor Betty all the way to the back of the reference section, to a corner full of economic-theory texts that hadn't been touched by human hands since the 1970s, before I mustered up the courage to speak. "Something's going on, and I'm not sure what to do."

Betty's gaze moved to my hands, and when I glanced down, I realized I was wringing them together so hard my knuckles were white. "What happened? You're scaring me."

She touched my arm, and I caught a fleeting glimpse of the crescent-moon scars in her palms. With her doe eyes, pale complexion, and vaguely melancholic air, Betty Cooper could have stepped right out of a painting by Vermeer.

But she also had a darker side.

We'd all seen her squeeze her hands into fists so tight her nails drew blood, and I had once watched her go full dark, no stars, with Chuck Clayton, holding his head underwater in a roiling hot tub. She'd scared me that night, and we'd all vowed to pull her back from the edge when she got too close . . . but just now I was grateful to have someone in my corner who was capable of dangerous things.

It hit me suddenly how much I'd changed over the past few years. My moral center was so askew that I was hoping for a little of Dark Betty's black magic to rub off on me. My father really *would* be proud.

The air in the library was hushed, ringing with silence between every cough and sniffle of the patrons on the other side of the towering shelves, but I looked over my shoulder nonetheless. At last, wordlessly, I pulled Poison Pen's envelope out of my clutch and pressed it into Betty's hands.

As she read the letter through, her eyes widened and the color drained from her face. "Wh-where did this come from? How . . . ?"

"Someone delivered it to the front desk at the Five Seasons, about thirty minutes ago." Goose bumps pebbled my skin as the library's air conditioner breathed down our necks. "Look what else came with it."

I gestured to the envelope, and Betty drew out the accompanying photograph. She did a double take as she compared it to my outfit and put two and two together. "This was . . . someone took a picture of you *today*?"

"They took a picture of me *this morning*, at the Five Seasons, and then dropped it at the concierge with a note saying they're watching me," I summarized hoarsely. Already I was starting to regret my choice of the library for our rendezvous; I'd thought the stillness, the warren of dusty shelves and forgotten tomes, would make it easier to hide. But I was wrong. The stifling quiet made even our softest whispers sound like screams. "Someone *knows*, B."

Her eyes scanning the photograph carefully, Betty murmured, "But how? You didn't . . . say anything to anyone, did you?"

"No!" I reclaimed the photo from her hands, trying not to look insulted. "I should hope it would be quite obvi that I would never." Lowering my voice even further, I hissed, "We made an agreement, and I have stuck by it."

"It wasn't an accusation, V."

"I'm sorry." Taking a deep breath, sucking in the chill air and the scent of dusty paper, I buried the envelope—photo and all—at the bottom of my bag. "This just has me rattled, I suppose. Anyway, you know there's a limited number of people I'd even trust enough with something like this . . . and those people already know."

Betty nodded, staring into the middle distance. "Do you think one of them might have . . ."

"Talked?"

"Sent this," she corrected me gravely, her eyes focusing again just like that, and I nearly recoiled. *This* was Dark Betty—a girl who could see the worst in everyone.

"No. No way." I shook my head vehemently. "What possible reason could they have for sending this? Who would, even as a prank?" Biting my lip, crossing my fingers behind my back, I asked, "Do you think maybe it could be just a prank?"

"I don't know." Betty stared at my clutch, like she could read the letter right through it. "'*Don't tell anyone*'? '*I'm watching you*'? It's over the top, but . . . that 'poor little rich girl' stuff feels really personal. And someone was waiting for you in the lobby?" She hugged herself, casting a glance around. Dust motes flecked the air, and high shelves blocked our view of the other patrons. "This *is* Riverdale. It's always safest to assume the worst and prepare for the . . . extra worst. Are you sure you weren't followed here?"

"I think so? I mean, I think I wasn't." Ice water raced through my veins, and I couldn't help a nervous laugh. "Don't take this the wrong way, B, but you're doing a really lousy job of telling me not to worry."

"I want to, honestly," she returned with a plaintive look—which only made it ten times worse, "but now you sort of have me convinced it's *not* a hoax. There's just too much at stake for this to be an inside job. Everyone has something to lose." Betty let out a troubled breath. "But it doesn't make sense as a bluff, either. I mean, how could Poison Pen make a *guess* this accurate? And if it's real, and this person really knows . . ."

My heart skipped a beat. Clasping my bestie's hands in my own, I implored, "I need your brain, Nancy Drew—that's why I took this chance. Help me figure out who's behind this, before . . . before the 'extra worst' can happen."

"You said someone left the note at the front desk of the Five Seasons. Did you ask—"

"Way ahead of you." I held up a hand. "I practically interrogated the concierge before I left for the library, and I got nowhere. The Pendergast event has taken over the hotel, and the staff is thoroughly overwhelmed. To hear the desk clerk tell it, he looked away for one instant, and when he looked back, there was an envelope sitting there."

"Okay, but that tells us something." Betty tilted her head, considering. "Poison Pen was there early enough to take that picture and had the time to print it out, come back, and wait around until the desk clerk was sufficiently distracted."

"It's a Saturday. In summer. Not to cast aspersions on your deductive prowess, but lots of people have that kind of time on their hands today."

Betty, bless her, was undaunted by the criticism. "Sure. But lots of people don't, and that letter didn't come from a stranger. It came from someone who *knows* you, V. Someone who seems to pretty seriously resent you." She bobbed her head, ponytail bouncing. "And someone who doesn't have a summer job with hours on Saturday."

"Or someone whose summer job is working at a hotel, or for the catering company a hotel contracted for a huge party on a Saturday," I pointed out wearily. "I personally sent an email blast to the entire Riverdale High listserv to recruit people for this little soiree—*event*," I corrected myself. Poison Pen's snide taunting—*"no doubt you prefer a word that's far more pretentious and grandiose than* party*"*—needled the back of my brain. Who hated me this much? "Even if that did narrow it down, it still doesn't tell us *who*."

"Or how," she returned immediately. "Are you absolutely sure there was no else in the parking garage that night?"

"Positive." It was the only thing I'd thought about on the walk to the library. "When I tell you I made those deputies do a thorough search, *believe me*, it was thorough."

"But what about before that? Couldn't someone have been there and then snuck out while you were calling the sheriff's office?"

"I . . ." For the millionth time in the past hour, I thought back to July Fourth. I remembered the distant *crack-boom* of fireworks, the way my footsteps scraped and clattered in the stairwell of the parking garage, the tomblike emptiness and swimming shadows. With a helpless gesture, I said, "Anything is possible. But I would swear the structure was completely deserted that night—my car was the only one parked on that entire floor!"

Betty's expression remained troubled. "But it doesn't make sense. Poison Pen claims to have 'proof,' but unless they were there, how would they know what happened? How could they even guess enough to connect it to . . . anything else?" Her hands tightened into fists, knuckles blanching. "Maybe the security camera—"

"It was down for the count." My tone was flat and firm. "A total KO. And the car was on the second floor, back from the railing. Even if someone had been walking by precisely then, they couldn't have seen anything. I'm sure of that—I checked." A knot started to form between my shoulder blades, and I tried to relax. "The only thing across from the garage on that side of the building was a gas station. There was no view."

"But they know," Betty murmured. "Or they know enough to guess. And if they do know, then why go after you, when there are—" She cut herself short, and our eyes met, a whole conversation happening in silence. Then she gave me a mirthless little smile. "Here's where I'd ordinarily ask if you have any enemies, but . . ."

"Give me a few days, and I'll narrow the list down to the top fifty likeliest suspects," I quipped. "This whole thing has me entirely unstrung. I'm supposed to give a speech at the party tonight that I haven't even written yet, and I've been trapped in that suite all day long with—" And just like that, it hit me. My eyes going huge, I gasped. "*B!* I know who's behind this!"

"Who?"

"I'll give you a hint." I crossed my arms, a tingle of anger heating my blood. "What 'Pen' do we know who is both a verified psychopath and a poison connoisseur?"

Betty's eyebrows hitched up. "You think *Penelope Blossom* sent that letter?"

"Who else?" I spread my hands. "This kind of vindictiveness and manipulation is exactly her cup of toxic tea. When she was posing as the Gargoyle King, she got people to drink cyanide, jump out windows, and attempt murder!" The knot between my shoulders receded. "She absolutely fits the bill. I can't believe I didn't think of her immediately!"

Sweeping past Betty, I marched for the front of the library, that tingle building to a roar. My bestie caught up with me just as I was bursting outside, and she put a hand on my elbow. "V, wait, what are you going to do?"

"Are you kidding? Life is way too short, and I am way too busy, to put up with this nonsense!" Fuming, I turned a glare in the direction of the Five Seasons, the upper stories just visible over the treetops. "I'm going back to the hotel, and I am going to put my four-inch stiletto heel on that miserable hag's throat. I am done being messed with!"

"Be careful!" Betty called out as I stormed away down the sidewalk. I was already rehearsing what I'd say, how I'd put Penelope Blossom in her place, and I didn't listen.

I should have.

Halfway back to the Five Seasons, I joined a crowd of people on a busy street corner, some waiting for the traffic signal to change, and others lingering around the adjacent bus stop for the number 4 to Southside. I was still angry, still thinking.

Penelope had been in the suite with us when the letter was dropped at the front desk, but that meant nothing; as the Gargoyle King, she'd recruited and commanded dozens of minions to do her dirty work. The crowd around me thickened, people bumping me as they jockeyed for position, but I barely noticed. Mentally, I relived the moment the note from "Poison Pen" was delivered to the suite—that redheaded vampire watching me from her chair. She must have felt so smug, waiting to see if I would crack right in front of her.

With a loud rumble, the number 4 bus appeared—late, as usual, and speeding to make up for lost time. As it hurtled for our corner, someone jostled me from behind, nudging me closer to the curb.

"Hey, watch—"

I didn't get to finish. A hand pressed against the small of my back . . . and *shoved*. The precarious heels of my Tom Ford sandals lost purchase on the pavement, and I flew forward, toppling over the curb and into the street—directly in the path of the oncoming bus.

CHAPTER FOUR

There was the blast of a horn and the squeal of brakes—all of it drowned out by the sound of my terrified screaming. The bus shuddered and groaned as its tires dug into the pavement, a flock of pigeons scattering into the air, and my life flashed before my eyes.

With a jolt, the massive vehicle came to a stuttering halt about eight feet shy of running me over. Where I fell was well ahead of the actual bus stop, and I probably hadn't truly been on the verge of getting flattened, but I was still sobbing and hyperventilating when the driver burst out through the folding doors, his face beet red. "What the hell is wrong with you, lady—you got a death wish or something?"

"I didn't . . . that wasn't . . . s-someone pushed me!" My voice trembled, and blood welled in a scrape along the side of my knee, but when I looked up at the crowd still gathered on the curb, all I saw were stunned, frightened expressions. And for once, of course, I recognized none of them. "Which one of you did it?"

Fear and anger made me sound deranged, and the crowd

shuffled back, eyes snapping away from me as each person decided to become uninvolved.

"*Which one of you did it?*" I repeated, shouting, scrambling to my feet. Right on cue, the traffic signal changed, and the crowd dispersed. Most of them flocked past me, heading for the opposite curb, while plenty more just . . . vanished, scattering in any direction that would take them away from the ranting girl in the street.

Also right on cue, my phone let out a little *ding* from inside my clutch, letting me know I had a text message.

Unknown ID:

I'm disappointed in you, VL. You had one job—don't tell—and the first thing you did was blab to Betty Cooper. I'm not surprised, though. You never seem to handle things without the help of someone smarter and stronger, do you? Well, too bad, princess, because the next assignment is worth 100 percent of your grade, and if you cheat? You WILL be roadkill.

Unknown ID:

Did you know that Senator Pendergast is having an affair with one of his top-level election campaign staffers? It's true. And tonight, both the Mrs. and the mistress will be under the same roof, at young Pernilla's engagement party. Pretty tacky, if you ask me, and a definite invitation for trouble. And that's where you come in.

Poor Mrs. Pendergast has no clue what's happening right under her nose, and I think you're just the girl to spill the beans. So tonight, when the champagne, music, and bonhomie are flowing, I want you to expose the senator in front of everyone. If you don't, I'll expose YOU. And in case you think I've been bluffing . . .

[Attachment1.jpg] [Attachment2.jpg] [Attachment3.jpg]

The next bus is coming fast, Ronniekins, but you get to decide who goes under the wheels. Senator P . . . or you and your friends?

∧∧∧

I was still shaking by the time I made it back to the Five Seasons, jumping at the sound of skidding tires, looking back every five steps to see who might be in my shadow. I knew Penelope wouldn't dare leave the Maple Club, but I'd already sent an embarrassingly clumsy text to Cheryl, asking about it. (Her reply: *Of course Mumsie is still here. I told her that whenever she wishes to leave I will happily deliver her to the sheriff myself, but unfortunately she has yet to take me up on the offer.*)

The knot between my shoulder blades was back, as large and dense as a fist, and the refrigerated lobby only made my skin go tight around it. Unable to help myself, I accessed the pictures Poison Pen had texted me, staring at them all over again. Grainy and grayscale, time-stamped July Fourth, they were still plain—and damning—enough.

Attachment 1: In which one Veronica Lodge swings a baseball bat at a security camera on the second floor of a parking garage.

Attachment 2: In which Veronica Lodge uses the same bat to smash the windshield of her own car.

Attachment 3: In which Veronica Lodge uses a can of spray paint to deface the hood of said car with a hideous, grinning skull.

It felt as though my chest had been scooped out when those images loaded on the screen. I *had* been careful. It was late, the garage was empty, I'd instructed my driver to park where I knew no one would see me when I returned later—where no one could possibly watch me from the ground. Approaching the security camera from behind, I'd struck it down from its perch, and I'd thought I was in the clear.

I hadn't considered the possibility of a traffic camera, mounted across the street, level with the second story of the parking structure. I hadn't considered the possibility that anyone would know enough, or care enough, to dig that deep.

Even the deputies I'd begged and harangued for help had been uninterested in doing more than the bare minimum.

"I have proof. I'm watching you."

That hadn't been a bluff . . . so I couldn't count on anything else about Poison Pen's threat to be a bluff, either.

Filing a false police report—vandalizing my own property and lying about it to the authorities—came with serious consequences I didn't want to deal with. But I also wouldn't be the first socialite to snap under the pressure of constant public scrutiny and act out. In the event that these pictures went public, well . . . I've spent my whole life watching wily criminals escape through loopholes, and I do know how to cry on cue.

Since we're being honest, I can afford lawyers who might convince a judge that letting me go to Switzerland for a while—for "treatment" for "exhaustion"—would be justice served. It would be an unpleasant storm to weather, but I could weather it.

The problem was the "and your friends" part. If Poison Pen pulled on this particular string, a lot more would unravel than just my personal plans for Barnard. Multiple futures hung in the balance, ones claimed by tooth and nail through bloody battles fought over the past year—and I was willing to risk none of them.

I'd spent so long at the library with Betty (and recovering from near-death by bus) that the Maple Club's suite was almost empty when I reached it, operations having already moved to the ballroom ahead of the event. The gift bags were arranged in rows on one of the tables, and Toni was rifling through them, furtively snatching out little white cards from each one.

She whirled when I stomped into the room, and then exhaled a shaky breath. "Please don't tell Cheryl. I love her to death—you *know* how much I love her—but she made an executive decision to include a patented 'Cheryl Blossom lip print' with each bag, and . . . I'm making an executive decision to sabotage her, because it's a terrible idea."

"A 'lip print'?" I cocked my head in confusion, and Toni turned one of the cards around, so I could see that it was exactly what it sounded like: Cheryl had kissed each little square of card stock, leaving behind an impression of her lips in her signature Chanel Rouge Allure shade. Making a wee "yikes" face, I said, "Carry on. Listen, do you happen to know where Penelope is?"

Toni pointed me to the sitting room—where I found Cheryl's mother casually filing her nails into sharp, spear-like points while listening to music from an old-fashioned record player. I slammed the door shut behind me and then ripped the needle off the spinning vinyl disc with a loud scratch and rounded on my quarry at last.

"You and I need to have a little chat," I announced through my teeth.

The woman gazed up at me with a cold, patient smile. "It's nice of you to finally make your reappearance, Veronica. We were all wondering what became of you."

"As if you don't know, you . . . you *succubus*!" Fury itched beneath my skin.

"I'm afraid I truly don't." Penelope's stenciled brows lifted. "But this has the unmistakable ring of an accusation."

"Whatever game you're playing? It ends now. *Tonight*." I swept my hands apart decisively. "No more messages. No more notes, no more texts, no more threats—or the one going under the next bus is *you*. Do you understand me?"

"Not in the least." She peered at me, eyes glimmering, and I realized that X-ray machine stare ran in the Blossom family. "Although I certainly wish I did. Whatever has you this agitated must be truly delicious."

For a moment, I was speechless, trying to figure her out. I was right about this—I *had* to be. Penelope Blossom was a consummate liar, I reminded myself, capable of bluffing her way out of just about anything.

"Notes and messages . . ." She knitted her fingers together. "Does this, perchance, have anything to do with that envelope you received this afternoon—the one that made you flee the Maple Club so abruptly?" Her expression was tranquil, reptilian. "Whatever did it have inside?"

"Don't do this," I snarled. "Don't pretend you don't know about this—it's got your claw prints all over it!"

"Veronica, dear, whatever it is you're going on about, I assure you it's got nothing to do with me." She gave an innocent shrug, that creepy smile still locked into place, and I shivered. "If you show me the messages you're talking about, though, perhaps I can help you figure out who sent them. Since you seem to believe we think alike."

She held out her hand, palm up, and I recoiled. Was this a trap? There was no way she was telling the truth—Penelope Blossom didn't know *how*. But she was so calm, her expression so fixed, that it was impossible to read her.

I opened my mouth, but I was saved from having to conjure a reply when the door banged back open behind me and Cheryl walked in. "Mumsie, please stop breathing so close to Veronica. Or perhaps just in general."

"Cheryl." Penelope greeted her daughter with a great, long-suffering sigh.

"Whatever poison you're pouring into my cohostess's ear, begone with it!" Cheryl flicked her hands at her mother in a shooing motion. "We have festivities to prepare for, and I won't have you wasting our time."

"Veronica came to me, dear," Penelope returned. "And I still have no idea why. It seems she's quite vexed over some correspondence she received, and she's decided that I'm to blame for it. I was merely asking her to explain herself."

"A very likely story!" And Cheryl was off to the races, locking horns with her mother in one of their frequent arguments— while my doubt and confusion tripled. If Penelope and Poison Pen were one and the same, she wouldn't dare make such an offhand mention of the messages I was getting. Not after having me pushed into traffic to teach me a lesson.

And then a chime sounded in my bag—my phone.

Unknown ID:

> I'd love to know what's got you so busy up there, but given your parting words to Betty, I have a pretty solid idea. Sorry, Ronnie—no cigar for you! Penelope wasn't a bad guess, but I'm afraid you're colder than the organs at the Farm.

Looking up, I stared at Penelope—but she was fully engaged in the quarrel with her daughter. Not only wasn't she secretly texting me, she barely even seemed aware of my presence at all anymore. If she had indeed hired some hoodlum to terrorize me, and she could resist so much as even a sidelong glance to enjoy my reaction when I received another one of her messages by proxy, then her self-control was truly unmatched.

My phone chimed again.

I'm getting bored down here, Ronnie. The ballroom is filling up, and the tea isn't going to spill itself, so hurry it up, okay? Your moment of truth approaches, and I want you to focus. I won't be happy until someone's life is ruined tonight, and if it's not Senator P's, then it will be yours.

Yet another message came in, filled with attached images, and my mouth went dry. They were high quality, shot at a seedy motel on the Southside, and they told a very clear story about the senator's infidelity.

Unknown ID:

If you had any doubts that I was telling you the truth about Pendergast's affair, now you have the evidence. Make the call, Ronnie, or I will—and we both know what's at stake if your secrets come out first . . .

CHAPTER FIVE

"For those of you who don't know him yet, let me tell you a little bit about my future son-in-law." A few hours later, the party in full swing, Senator Pendergast stood in the middle of the ballroom. He was on the final lap of an interminable toast he was making to his daughter and her fiancé, working the crowd like the seasoned politician he was.

"Hayes Huxley is a local boy, born and raised right here in this humdinger of a town. Our former mayor, Sierra McCoy, is in attendance tonight . . . she spoke at his graduation from Riverdale High just a few years back, encouraging public service and civic responsibility. Madame Mayor, you might be the very reason that Hayes joined the Rockland County Sheriff's Office!" There was a scattering of applause before Pendergast reached the punch line: "I don't know if I should thank you for that or tell you off!"

The butterflies in my stomach had grown into pterodactyls, and I kept compulsively drying my sweaty palms on the black skirt of my Marchesa cocktail dress. I'd been circling the ballroom like a shark, in near-constant motion, scanning every face in the crowd. The guests included anyone in town who wielded a bit of influence, and I recognized too many—my own wretched parents among them. As for the staff, the hotel had hired a number of my former classmates at Riverdale High to pass canapés and drinks.

Once again, I was surrounded by familiar faces . . . any of whom could have been Poison Pen.

A hundred times or more, I told myself I couldn't go through with what I was about to do—but I had no choice. Poison Pen was out there . . . and whoever they were, they weren't playing around. There was no time to think of a brilliant plan B after I falsely accused Penelope Blossom of being my tormentor; my time was up.

One of us, either Pendergast or me, was going down in flames. And I was the one holding the match.

"I'm kidding!" the senator continued, grinning with red-faced, avuncular charm so his audience would know it was true. "Everyone here knows I have a reputation for being tough on crime. At the heart of my current campaign to become the next governor of this great state is an initiative to increase support for our law enforcement agencies. Together, we need to crack down on lawbreakers, and good men like Hayes Huxley are how it'll get done."

Stronger applause. Everyone knew what kind of crime was rampant in Riverdale, and we were all eager to see it stop. Serial killers, organ thieves, drug runners, *anonymous blackmailers.*

Someone in a catering uniform handed me a glass of champagne, and it took all my willpower to keep from downing it like a shot.

"In fact, just this past June, Hayes helped make the streets of Riverdale a little bit safer." Pendergast's folksy smile was stretched across his face like a billboard. "When a volunteer for my campaign was mugged in Sketch Alley—stabbed with a switchblade and robbed of cash donations—it was Hayes and his partner who made the arrest."

Cheryl shot me a dark glance from across the room. Not only did we know the truth behind these misleading words, but we also knew a host of related facts that would shock the room. I couldn't take it anymore. With a flick of my wrist, I guzzled the champagne and was snatching a replacement off the tray of a passing waiter before I'd even finished swallowing.

"So here is to my daughter, Pernilla, and her future husband!" The senator held his champagne flute aloft, and a boisterous round of cheers filled the room. I drained my second glass just as Pendergast said, "And now I yield the floor to the lovely Veronica Lodge. Please show your appreciation, friends, because she and Cheryl Blossom are responsible for every part of this little shindig!"

I almost choked.

With the microphone in my hand, hot lights blazing in my eyes—and the knowledge of what was about to happen churning in my stomach—I began to speak. "As Polonius said in

Hamlet, 'Brevity is the soul of wit.' So, to avoid appearing utterly witless, I shall be brief." There was laughter, but I barely heard it. "Cheryl and I were thrilled to organize this event, and it is my personal pleasure to introduce the following film reel celebrating the courtship of the happy couple."

My Gianvito Rossi pumps wobbled as I hurried back into the shadows. I held my breath as the lights went down and a projector linked to my laptop started to throw images against a screen on the wall. The music was beautiful, and the first few photos—of Pernilla Pendergast and Hayes Huxley eating ice cream, hiking in Fox Forest, standing at the top of the Empire State Building—drew affectionate cooing from the crowd.

But the mood spoiled quickly when the first pictures of Patrick Pendergast and his mistress popped up.

"What the hell is this?" The senator jolted from his seat as the images shifted from him and a young blond arriving at a Southside no-tell motel to them entering a room with crooked numbers on the door. "*What is this?* Where did these pictures come from?"

"Patrick?" Mrs. Pendergast stared, her face pale, and I grabbed the closest glass that still had champagne in it . . . but I could hardly open my throat for air, let alone alcohol. Murmurs raced around the room, building to a din.

"*Shut this off!*" Pendergast shouted as the film reel continued, his affair revealed to his family, his friends, and his inner circle by more photos, shot through the motel room's venetian blinds. *"Shut it off! Shut it off NOW!"*

The din escalated. Pernilla started to cry, and Mrs. Pendergast threw her drink in her husband's face, screaming obscenities. It was Cheryl who finally sprinted to my laptop, ripping the cord out and ending the torture. She gaped at me from across the room—a question, or maybe an accusation . . . but all I could do was stare blankly back.

Our big event, the party of the year, was collapsing around us. The Pendergast women fled the room in tears, and guests got to their feet, dispensing with any pretense at decorum. The senator stood alone, transfixed—breathing hard, beet red, and soaked in champagne.

All I could hope was that the secrets of July Fourth would stay hidden now. For good.

∧∧∧

Unknown ID:

Nice job, Ronniekins! I knew you'd make the right choice.

Veronica:

Go to hell

Unknown ID:

See you there 😲

Poor Senator Pendergast. I wonder how he feels about this "humdinger of a town" now, after getting hit upside the head with the Maple Club. And I wonder how our girl Ronnie is going to play off this wee catastrophe! After all the work she's done to wriggle out from under Hiram's boot to prove she can succeed on her own, it sure would be sad if her dreams fell apart because of someone else's misdeeds.

Not that she'd know anything about that.

While Veronica may enjoy quoting Shakespeare, I prefer the strategical genius of Sun Tzu: Know thyself, know thy enemy. After all, it doesn't matter how outclassed you are if you can find your opponent's pressure points and dig your fingers into them.

If you have the will and the tenacity to fight <u>dirty</u>.

Hiram Lodge knows it, and on the rare occasion she's being honest, Veronica knows it, too. But then, her greatest strength has always been her greatest liability: her loyalty to her friends.

You can't blame her. After growing up in that snake pit of a household, and getting cast aside and cold-shouldered by the circle of fickle frenemies she ran with back in Manhattan, what does she have but her friends here in Riverdale? What would she have left if her secret got out and the blowback brought terrible consequences upon the people she cares about most?

Lucky for her, she won't have to find out—yet, anyway. I promised not to tell as long as she did what I asked, and she danced like a good little marionette. It was so fun, I'm almost sad to let her off the hook.

Lucky for me, there are plenty of puppets to play with in this town's twisted toy box.

I'm not the only one in our humdinger of a town who likes to investigate the crimes of others—who learns about shady dealings and can't rest until they're brought to the light of day. Maybe it's high time that I moved on to someone who can truly appreciate the power of the written word . . .

—Poison Pen

PART TWO
JUGHEAD JONES
SUNDAY

CHAPTER SIX

Religion and the Jones family never really mixed well together. When I was growing up, Mom didn't have much use for church, socially or spiritually—and as for my dad? After a Saturday night out, he did all his praying to the porcelain god. Once he got his act together, the institution he turned to for guidance and comfort was the Southside Serpents.

You might think a motorcycle gang headquartered in a dive bar would be a lousy influence on a guy with alcohol dependency problems. And . . . okay, you'd be right. But it turns out my dad thrives in leadership roles, so every Sunday morning—instead of sleeping off a hangover—he'd be out in front of our trailer, working on his bike.

Even after he "retired" from the Serpents (and I use scare quotes because, mark my words, *a Serpent never sheds its skin*), the whole automotive-upkeep thing remained his weekend ritual. When I became a Serpent myself, I started joining my dad on Sunday mornings, our bikes side by side while we checked filters, changed fluids, replaced parts.

Working on my engine made a lot of the world disappear. It

was just me and the machine, problems that needed solving, and a search for answers. Maybe it wasn't as exciting as unmasking a killer, but completing any puzzle is at least a little rewarding.

Not to get all *Zen and the Art of Motorcycle Maintenance*, but . . . it turned out there was something really Zen about the art of motorcycle maintenance.

This particular Sunday in early August, of course, was a somewhat different story. Since Dad had taken off with Jellybean, there was no tradition to share anymore. There was no one to roust me from my couch-bound slumber, to pour molasses-thick coffee down my throat or harangue me outside while I grumbled good-naturedly about wanting to sleep in for once. There was no one to offer me unsolicited criticism about the shoddy job I'd done of replacing a cracked feed pipe or realigning a crankshaft.

There was no one at all.

And yet early Sunday morning, I was out in the driveway of the Coopers' house, anyway (or maybe it's the Cooper-Jones house now, or the *Smith*-Cooper-Jones house—it's hard to keep track), with grease up to my elbows. My bike didn't even need any particular work, but still I spent hours scrubbing valves that were already clean and polishing spotless chrome, my shirt stuck to my back with sweat. After the year I'd had, I wasn't about to give up on one more thing that made my life feel normal.

Maybe that sounds depressing—me sweltering in the midday heat, doing work that didn't need to be done, just to feel like my life hadn't hit the reset button once again, as soon as things were finally going right—but . . . well, okay, actually, it *was* sort of depressing.

Not having Jellybean around was bittersweet, to say the least, my feelings a jumble of love and sadness and betrayal; even when she and Mom took off for Toledo, I'd always had my dad around. We were the Jones Boys, and I still thought of us that way. Even if his absence hurt like a phantom limb, sticking to the routine made me feel closer to him somehow, just the same. It made my chaotic life a little less uncertain, and *that* was worth every unnecessary ache and pain I felt as I toiled away.

When I'd finished all the odd work I could make a credible excuse to do, I packed up my tools, mopped my brow, and headed for the house.

⌁⌁⌁

The impression I get from people who do go to church on Sundays is that heaven is an eternity of white robes and miniature harps, like a sixties folk band trapped forever in a bounce house in the sky. For me, heaven is a five-stack of my dad's chocolate-chip pancakes drenched in Blossom Maple Syrup, served up with a mug of coffee dense enough to walk on.

The Jones family never had much in the way of legacies to pass down, but my dad's recipe for breakfast decadence was worth more than the entire Baxter Brothers empire, as far as I was concerned. The pancakes never turned out quite the same when I made them, and I hadn't yet figured out what I was doing wrong—but just like motorcycle maintenance, the journey was more important than the destination.

I was setting out all the ingredients I needed for a late breakfast, lining up flour, eggs, and chocolate chips (extra this time, because why not?) when the doorbell rang. For a moment, I just stood there, waiting—until I remembered that I was the only one in the house.

Stomach growling at the interruption, I headed for the front hall. But when I opened the door, the porch was empty. Sun dazzled on the glass of curbside cars, and a warm breeze carried the scent of fresh-cut lawns, but the only sign of life I could see out there was plant matter.

I looked down, instinctively expecting a new videocassette delivery from a copycat psycho . . . and blinked. At my feet, dead center on the Smith-Cooper-Jones welcome mat, was a plain white envelope with my name across the front. When I picked it up, I found the flap sealed with a circle of red wax, stamped with an ornate double *P*.

Dear Jughead,

My, it's been quite a year! SATs and college inter-
views, forging new relationships and ending old
ones, landing book deals and faking homicides.
And through it all, you've managed to stay true to
who you are: a self-pitying, self-aggrandizing,
self-styled loner.

Jughead Jones, the Jack Kerouac of Riverdale...
if Riverdale was Sesame Street and Kerouac was
Grover with a tattoo. News flash, Juggie: A hat isn't
a personality. You're so determined to be misunder-
stood that you can't even grasp how generic you
actually are. What kind of outcast is friends with
all the most popular kids in town? You need a wake-
up call, Diet James Dean, and—lucky for you—I'm
just the one to deliver it.

I've been paying attention, Jug, and I know you
better than you know yourself. For all your posturing, you're still just an ordinary boy, making
terrible decisions and trying to justify them by
blaming forces beyond your control.

Fact: On the night of July Fourth, you stole a
car over in Greendale.

You are quite naughty for that, by the way! Oh,
you had your reasons (and, believe me, Forsythe, I

know what those reasons are), but will that matter
to the new sheriff? Word on the street is he can't
afford to pick and choose which laws he enforces
these days. If he tried to cut his son's friend slack
for a little grand theft auto, he'd be flogged in the
public square—especially if an anonymous source
sent proof to the mayor, the media, and our very own
fire-breathing, anti-crime superhero, Senator
Pendergast.

And if you go down, FPJ3, what happens to the
others implicated in your crime?

I'm willing to keep my mouth shut about it . . .
for now. But I want you to consider what my confidence is worth, because I am not quiet by nature.
You'll be hearing from me again soon, Juggie. And
in the meantime? I expect you to keep this note
between you and me. I waited until you went inside
to drop this off, so you know I'm watching you. If
you tell anyone we've been in touch, there will be
consequences.

—Poison Pen

CHAPTER SEVEN

I read it three times over, my blood pressure dropping, my fingers going cold despite the rising temperature of the August air. The street remained empty, birds darting overhead . . . but I felt *watched*. Even more acutely than when those videotapes first turned up, our front door in the crosshairs.

Someone knew about July Fourth.

The makings of a pancake brunch still waited on the kitchen counter, but I barely noticed, grabbing my messenger bag and leather jacket, moving on autopilot. The contents of that insidious letter sparked in my brain like a downed power line— *"you know I'm watching you"*—and I suddenly couldn't handle being alone in the house a minute longer. I rushed back to the front hall and threw open the door again . . . and nearly slammed into a figure standing on the porch.

I let out a frightened yelp, and at the same moment the person on the porch screamed—and *glared* at me. *"Jughead Jones,* what is *wrong* with you? You scared me half to death!"

"Ms. Smith?" Betty's mother blocked the doorway, arms loaded with bulging paper sacks, and I blinked. "Sorry!

I'm sorry, I thought . . . I was . . ." But I trailed off, not sure how to finish what I was saying—not sure what I was saying to begin with. Behind her, the street was still bright, peaceful, and empty. "Did you . . . see anyone outside just now?"

"Did I *see anyone outside?*" she repeated, wrinkling her nose, like the question was absurd. "No. It's a million degrees out today; everyone with any sense is hiding." Then, cocking an imperious brow, she asked, "Are you going to help me with these groceries?"

It was an offer I couldn't exactly refuse. My relationship with Betty's mom had always been . . . well, let's say "strained," but I couldn't deny that she'd been gracious in letting me remain under her roof after the dramatic end of her relationship with my father. Reluctantly, I accepted one of the bags and started following her back to the kitchen, a worried lump expanding in my throat.

"I assume you've already heard about what happened at the Five Seasons last night," Alice remarked out of nowhere, like it was a subject she couldn't wait to bring up.

"Uh, the basics, anyway. A highly anticipated event ending in unmitigated catastrophe?" Nerves thinned my voice, that letter eating my thoughts like radioactive waste. "Sounds like an average weekend in Riverdale."

"It was a journalist's dream come true." Her eyes glittered. "I got my cell phone out just in time to catch Mrs. Pendergast calling the senator a 'lying, no-account dirtbag' and tossing her champagne in his face."

"Do rich people really do that?" Despite myself, and the paranoid itch under my skin, I couldn't help but comment, "Seems like such a waste."

"Money turns people into children," Alice snorted. Then: "But I had a fantastic view of the whole thing, and RIVW *tripled* their offer on the footage when I told them competing networks were interested!"

"Um . . . lucky you?" I set my bag down on the kitchen counter and shifted my weight, shooting a look back toward the door—desperate to leave, but unsure how to make good my escape without being overtly rude.

"I feel just terrible for poor Veronica, though," Alice continued with a demonstratively empathic sigh, oblivious to my tone. "She says she has no idea how the slideshow was compromised, but apparently she left her laptop unattended all afternoon while running errands." There was a note of judgment in her voice, but if she was going to say more, she stopped when she finally noticed my riding leather. "Were you going somewhere?"

Her gaze dropped then to my messenger bag, and I gripped the strap so tightly the rough fabric hurt the palms of my hands. What would happen to my living situation if Betty's mother found out what I'd done? If she found out *why*? Babbling, I gave the first excuse that came into my head. "Yeah, sorry.

I'm . . . heading to Pop's. I promised Archie I'd meet him today."

For a moment, she just stared at me, her eyes flinty—and a hideous thought blossomed in my mind. *What if Alice wrote the letter?* She'd never liked me. What if, after everything she'd lost this year, she'd finally lost her mind, too? But then she sniffed, gesturing sharply to the flour, eggs, and chocolate still sitting out. "Were you planning to just leave those there while you gallivant around with Archie? *Honestly*, Jughead—"

She began grumbling about my carelessness, but I barely even heard her as I stashed the ingredients away, relief melting my thoughts—and then I was out the door, my pace just shy of a run.

My bike started up with a healthy growl, and the tires burned rubber as I raced up the street. There still wasn't a soul in sight . . . but I felt eyes boring into my back like a deadly corkscrew the whole way.

CHAPTER EIGHT

Once upon a time, July Fourth meant ice cream with Archie and Betty at the bandstand in Pickens Park; tracing my name in the air with a fizzling sparkler while Fred Andrews threw burgers on the grill; a ceremonial showing of *Independence Day* down at the Twilight Drive-In, cheering at all the right times.

But that was then. Now the Twilight was gone, and so was Fred Andrews, and any happy memories left from my childhood had a tendency to rot the moment I dug them up. I'd stopped making the effort. After all, what is nostalgia but selective amnesia—a gauzy, ego-friendly image of the past?

Tom Keller was our sheriff again, tasked with ensuring the safety and welfare of several hundred Riverdale citizens, who would spend the day drinking before crowding together in Pickens Park to set off a bunch of exploding rockets. Too much could go wrong. This would be the first real Fourth of July celebration since the death of Jason Blossom, and the mayor needed an unqualified success.

Which meant Tom Keller required every warm body he could get—by persuasion or force—to make sure peace was kept in Riverdale. And he wasn't above reminding me that I owed my community, especially after all the trouble I'd caused with my faked murder. If I hadn't already been deputized once, back when the Serpents helped take down the Gargoyles, maybe I could have argued against him. As things stood, however, I was on the hook.

But making sure no one burned the pavilion down, or lost their hand to a homemade firecracker, wasn't my only responsibility for the evening. As dusk first settled on our cozy little town, an hour before I was supposed to play the white knight in Pickens Park, I was dressed in black and riding shotgun on a clandestine trip to Greendale.

Only a handful of people knew what I was up to—that I was on my way to steal a car—and why.

The last threads of sunlight had just vanished over the tree-tops as my literal partner in crime and I reached the outskirts of Greendale, rumbling over a set of railroad tracks and passing into a derelict neighborhood that made Riverdale's old Southside look upscale. There was a scrapyard on the edge of town where I'd purchased automotive parts before, and they always had cars on the lot in various states of disrepair. They'd come in whole and get picked clean over time, harvested for parts like Edgar Evernever's followers.

The scrapyard also had a joke of a security system.

We pulled to the curb at an intersection two blocks away, by a wide cross street with clear sight lines in four directions. With the engine still running, I turned to my partner. "You know the drill. Eyes and ears open, and if you see anything, text my burner. If it's the cops—"

"Tap the horn three times, and then take off. If I don't hear from you within fifteen minutes, I head back to Riverdale. Alone." A smile, a sideways look. "See? I do know the drill."

"Thanks for this," I said, tugging on my gloves and pulling my watch cap low. "I'm not anticipating any trouble, but . . . this isn't even the hard part."

My lookout nodded briefly. "Let's hope everything goes smoothly—for everyone."

"In Riverdale? Don't tempt fate." Grabbing my little bag of tricks, I slipped out of the car, jogging for the scrapyard. My steps were soundless, and I clung to the shadows . . . but we were alone.

The job took less time than I'd expected. The scrapyard had a perimeter fence mounted with cameras, but they were all dummies, and the gate was secured with a chain that yielded easily to my bolt cutters. The dog I was supposed to beware of was fourteen years old; he barked once, and then wagged his tail when I tossed him a couple of Pop's hamburgers—laced with a mild sedative pilfered from Alice Smith's medicine cabinet.

While Cerberus dozed, I found a car that was in good order, save for a missing distributor cap and rear tire—both of which were easy to find replacements for—and then it was just a matter of jimmying the lock and hot-wiring the engine. Essential life skills every Serpent learns, sooner or later.

As I exited the lot, my lookout and I flashed our headlights at each other—*mission accomplished*—and then left in separate directions. Within half an hour, I'd be at Pickens Park, back straight and face scrubbed, confiscating bottle rockets from twelve-year-olds. I would never see that stolen car again, and if everything went according to plan, it would be found shortly and the scrapyard would get their property back.

The perfect crime. In and out, no witnesses.

Or so I'd thought.

ᴧᴧᴧ

The air in the Chock'Lit Shoppe was a bracing just-above-zero, and I nearly gasped when I walked through the door. I always wear my jacket for protection when I ride, and now my T-shirt was soaked through. I reached for my hat, but it wasn't only because my hair was a damp, sweaty mess that I paused before I put it on again.

"News flash, Juggie: A hat isn't a personality."

I knew people thought my hat was weird and that I was weird for wearing it. I knew they thought I wore it for no reason other than *being* deliberately weird. And . . . what could I say? On some level, they were right. But people had been looking at me like that my whole life, even before the hat.

They looked at me like a kid from the Southside, like a kid who lived in a trailer with a drunken gang leader for a dad and a foulmouthed brawler for a mom. They looked at me like I was poor and it was catching. I was a freak, an often-unwashed mass who didn't understand the things they talked about—video games, concerts, shows—because they were all luxuries I couldn't afford.

They made fun of me for not fitting in, and when I tried to figure out how, they made fun of me for that, too. So I stopped trying, and I embraced being "Diet James Dean." My hat is my freak flag, and I fly it with pride.

I put it on.

"Well, what do you know?" Pop smiled at me from behind the counter. "It's my favorite customer."

"You can't fool me, Pop." Dropping onto a stool, I peeled my shirt from my chest and let the circulating air blow down my sternum. "All your customers are your favorite."

"That's not true." He was indignant. "Hiram Lodge eats here sometimes."

I couldn't help but chuckle. This was about as close to trash talk as Pop Tate got. He confirmed my order—which was easy enough, as it was always the same—and set to preparing it. On a Sunday afternoon, the place wasn't empty, but the only people I knew were wave-across-the-room friends. So I reached into my messenger bag, fingers closing on the envelope that had been left by Poison Pen.

"On the night of July Fourth, you stole a car over in Greendale."

Every fiber of my being itched to reread that letter, to analyze it: the word choices, the handwriting, the paper. Somebody bought sealing wax and a personalized stamp; the envelope was a perfect square and the paper cut to size, so a simple fold would fit it neatly inside. Even if the items were purchased online, even if there was no way to trace the buyer, it still said something about the person who made those choices.

In another timeline, I would have called Betty to help me brainstorm. She would take one look and Veronica Mars her way to some logical conclusion. But things were complicated . . . and an order is an order.

"If you tell anyone we've been in touch, there will be consequences."

I'd lived in Riverdale too long to treat any threat as idle, to dismiss any danger—no matter how absurd or unlikely—out of hand. The problem was that I wasn't the only one whose future would hang by a thread if Poison Pen could prove what they clearly—somehow, impossibly—seemed to know.

"What happens to the others implicated in your crime?"

No doubt about it, I was in trouble. Again.

"Jug?"

The sound of my name brought me up short, and I jerked my hand out of the messenger bag like I'd been caught stealing from the till. Standing in the doorway, the bell still swinging above his head, was Archie Andrews. In that same other time-line, I'd have been thrilled to see him.

"Hey, Archie," I said, moving my bag so he could sit down next to me, grateful at least that his presence meant I hadn't technically lied to Betty's mother after all.

"I'm glad I ran into you, man." He clapped a hand on my

shoulder, his knuckles bruised but his smile beaming. "I haven't seen you all week! What've you been up to?"

"Writing, mostly." I answered honestly, but my throat swarmed with words desperate to spill out. Betty would have been the first person I'd gone to about that letter—if I thought it was safe—but Archie would have been the second.

After all, no matter what the message portended, they both needed to know about it.

Maybe if I could figure out who was behind this, maybe if I could confront them—determine what they *wanted*—then this whole episode could be over before it had the chance to blow up into something truly catastrophic.

"It's so great that you're really getting a chance to follow your dream, Jug." The sincerity in Archie's expression was warm and familiar. "You deserve it. After all the work you put in these past few years . . . your dad must be really proud of you."

"Yeah, he's thrilled. I'm the first Jones man in generations to head somewhere after high school that isn't prison. Or the military. Or a military prison." With a laugh, I added, "Can you imagine me in the military? I'd get court-martialed for sarcasm."

"Within a week," Archie agreed, grinning ear to ear. "I definitely think you picked the right path, Jug."

"Thanks, man. And, hey, here's to both our futures." I raised an imaginary glass, and we made an imaginary toast. "The past is done, and you're going to have your best year yet, just wait."

"You know, I actually thought about enlisting once before." Archie hesitated. "It was when my uncle Frank was staying with us. He talked about his tours of duty like the only time he knew what he was doing and where he belonged. It sounded like a relief, given what I was going through."

"Let me guess: The dream died when a mercenary the size of Mount Whitney tried to shot-put you through the lounge at Riverdale High?" I hadn't been there the day it happened, but I'd heard Kevin Keller tell the story multiple times, with varying degrees of embellishment.

"Believe it or not, no," Archie returned with a grin. "It was when I thought about who would run the community center while I was gone, and who would look in on my mom. I realized that I wanted to do those things." He gave a helpless little shrug. "But my mom has Brooke now, the center isn't doing that great, and . . . I don't know. Everything's changed so much this year. Maybe I need to make some changes, too, after all."

"Well, whatever you end up doing, your dad would be proud of you, you know," I told him. He looked so grave that I wanted to ask what was on his mind, but we were interrupted before I could.

"Afternoon, Archie," Pop said as he slid my order across the counter, a maraschino cherry the size of a candied apple sinking into my milk shake. "You hungry?"

"Starving." He clutched his stomach theatrically. "Can I get some onion rings, a cheeseburger, and . . . some more onion rings? Oh, and put on a huge pot of coffee, too—I've got a lot of work to do, and I'll probably be here for a while."

Pop lifted his brows. "That sounds serious."

"It is. I burned all my midnight oil, and now I guess I have to burn some of my early-afternoon oil, too." Archie smiled gamely, but it looked stiff. I knew he needed summer school credits in order to graduate, and I wondered how it was going . . . but he never seemed to want to talk about it, so I'd learned to stop asking.

"My goodness." Planting his hands on his hips, Pop shook his head. "When I think what filthy little imps the two of you once were, carving your names into my countertop and making yourselves sick on hot fudge . . . and now you're both grown up. An entrepreneur and a promising writer. I can hardly believe it."

"Hey," Archie protested, "you told us we could carve our names into that counter!"

"Yeah, and you had it replaced, like, two weeks later!" Jerking my thumb at the parking lot, I added, "Besides, I'm still a no-good hooligan. I drive a motorcycle and everything."

"A proud tradition for writers with a subversive side, such as yourself." There was a definite twinkle in Pop's eye. "William Burroughs had a motorcycle, didn't he?"

"No, he's the one who accidentally killed his wife playing William Tell," I answered, faster than I could see my own words coming. "You're thinking of Jack Kerouac."

Pop and Archie continued to volley back and forth, teasing each other as a means of remembering times past . . . but I was stuck again in the cold, uncomfortable present. *"Jughead Jones, the Jack Kerouac of Riverdale."*

Who was Poison Pen? The question screamed inside my thoughts, drowning out everything else. The insults in that letter were personal—and *mean*. They'd been written by someone with a grudge, someone who didn't want just to blackmail me but to make me suffer all the possible fates my imagination could devise.

"I want you to consider what my confidence is worth." An unspecified cost, a blank check that I would fill in over and over until I was contacted with specific terms. And the price of silence could be paid a million ways: money, information, illegal acts . . . Poison Pen could demand a "favor," and I'd be right back where I was sophomore year, when—

It hit me like a thunderbolt, and I jerked up from the stool so fast I banged the counter, nearly sending my milk shake to the floor. Archie glanced over, startled by whatever he saw in my face. "Jug? Everything okay?"

"No. I mean, yes!" My scattered thoughts were diving together, forming a stark picture, and I slung the strap of my messenger bag across my shoulder. "I just remembered I . . .

forgot about my laundry. Alice Smith will go full Alice Cooper if she comes home and all my clothes are still sitting in the dryer."

Pop refused payment for the food I'd barely touched, and I was out the door a second later, ripping off my hat and jamming my helmet on as I made a beeline for my bike. I knew exactly who had authored the letter in my bag, and I even knew where to find them.

It was time Poison Pen heard from *me*.

CHAPTER NINE

Poison Pen could demand a "favor," and I'd end up right back where I was sophomore year, when . . . Penny Peabody—the "Snake Charmer"—made me deliver a crate full of drugs to an address in Greendale as payment for her consultation on my father's case.

The tires of my bike howled as I sped toward Sweetwater River, trees forming a quilted canopy overhead, with maple leaves as big as catcher's mitts soaking up the August heat. Archie and Pop were welcome to the past; I didn't want it anymore.

When the investigation into Jason Blossom's murder turned up evidence against my dad, he'd been arrested. Frightened, vulnerable, and utterly alone, I had turned to a Serpent with a decidedly forked tongue for help: Penny Peabody—PP— *Poison Pen.*

I was furious with myself for not seeing the connection from the start. On our very first encounter, she'd recognized my desperation and naïveté, and instead of abiding by the sacred code of our gang, she had played me for a sucker.

After I became the Serpent King, she'd joined the Ghoulies, instigating bloody turf wars and running protection rackets against my friends; she'd tracked Archie and me to Toledo after he escaped from juvie, attacking us to claim the bounty on my best friend's head. The night Jellybean was kidnapped by the Gargoyles, Penny even tried to kill my mother in a vicious duel.

Gripping my handlebars, I leaned forward, exploding out of the trees as I reached the bridge. Sunlight glazed the water below as I flew across, and the air smelled rich and green . . . but all I saw was red.

Penny's grudge against me was personal—as was her connection to Greendale, where she had been running drugs for years. (And where I'd banished her to, once upon a time, after slicing the Serpent tattoo off her forearm.) Her multiple gang affiliations meant she could have spies everywhere, willing to make deliveries and report back. Not for nothing, the Gargoyles had worn masks. When their leader was exposed and defeated, the ones who weren't captured went to ground. Who knew how many were still out there?

But more to the point: Penny Peabody—*PP*—had already blackmailed me once.

Hurtling over the railroad tracks at the edge of town, racing through a stretch of shuttered businesses—motels, a bait shop, a pizza place once called Gina's—I slowed the bike. There was an intersection up ahead, at which a right turn would take me directly to the scrapyard where I'd stolen that car. Right on the Snake Charmer's turf. I'd let dummy cameras, shadows, and a year's worth of sleeping dogs convince me that there was no risk. But somehow, she'd made me.

Somehow she'd figured out the entire scheme.

Blazing through the intersection, I finally stopped my bike outside a place called the Devil's Bargain. It was a beer-and-billiards joint on the bad side of town (which was saying something for Greendale), with a damaged sign and windows caked in grime. The door was propped open with a cinder block, and I took that as an invitation.

Dark and humid, the bar stank of musty water and the stomach contents of drunks who didn't make it to the bathroom in time. Felt was peeling up on the pool tables, dangling bulbs cast sallow light from their metal shades, and speakers lost in the peripheral gloom played dreary music just a few BPMs too slow.

It was an even dingier dive than the Whyte Wyrm, the Serpents' old Southside headquarters, and . . . well, okay, yeah. A part of me was giddy that Penny had ended up in a dump like this.

"You can't come in here." An ugly guy with greasy hair and ill-fitting jeans emerged from a rectangle of darkness near the bar that I assumed to be a hallway.

Glancing over my shoulder, I feigned innocence. "The door was open."

"Not what I meant." Ugly cracked his knuckles, his nasty grin taking on some added menace. "*Serpents* ain't welcome here. *Jughead Jones*."

"Ah." I gave a modest shrug. "My reputation precedes me."

"And your butt is gonna precede your face if you don't get out of my bar in the next thirty seconds."

Pursing my lips, I tried to puzzle this one through. "Sorry, I don't mean to be obtuse, but . . . what does that mean? To 'precede' is to 'go before,' so are you trying to say you're going to throw me out, butt-first?"

"What I'm saying, is," he began with an infuriated hiss, yanking a switchblade from his hip pocket and flicking it open, "you'd best be leaving unless you want my knife to *precede* its way through your pencil neck."

"Okay." I took a few cautious steps to the side, backing into a billiard table, the man's blade looking admittedly deadly in his confident grip. "The word you're looking for here is 'proceed' and not 'precede,' but your meaning is clear enough."

"Ten seconds," he intoned, coming closer.

But on the lumpy green felt behind me was a long wooden pool cue. Like any good gang leader entering enemy territory, I'd clocked it when I first walked through the door, and now I snatched it up in practiced hands. My time at Stonewall Prep hadn't been good for much, but at least I'd learned the art of fencing.

With three strikes, I had Ugly and his knife on the floor at my feet. I was almost disappointed by how easy it was. As I scooped up the blade, slipping it into my pocket, I said, "Tell the Snake Charmer I want to see her."

"She's not here," he managed through gritted teeth, clutching the wrist I'd struck first with the cue's lead-weighted end.

"I don't believe you." I twirled my weapon—not as a threat, just because it's actually kind of fun. "But even if she's not here right now, I'll bet she shows up within about five minutes. Call her."

It was an easy bet to make. If Penny really did have eyes on me, her own or someone else's, then she likely already knew I'd entered her territory. Hell, if she was the one following me, then I'd led her here myself.

"I ain't calling nobody." Ugly spat onto the already-filthy floor. "But I *will* get my boys down here, and they'll take you apart—piece by piece."

"If you're not calling anybody, how are you supposed to get your boys here?" I inquired, leaning on the cue like a walking stick. "Homing pigeon? Telegram? Do they still send telegrams?"

Ugly was glaring at me balefully, perhaps trying to think his way through the little conundrum he'd created for himself, when another voice came from just beyond that dark doorway beside the bar.

"For Pete's sake, Ajax, stop embarrassing yourself." And then, stepping from the shadows, blond hair pulled back to show off her studded eye patch, Penny Peabody revealed herself at last. "If this little rodent wants to talk to me that bad, then fine. We'll talk."

∿∿∿

"You got ten minutes, Jones." It was her opening statement when we sat down, facing off over a scarred table in a corner by the jukebox. Ugly was behind the bar, watching us while he talked on the phone. "Ajax is probably calling his 'boys' right now, and they'll bring tire irons, so say whatever you came to say and then get out of my bar."

"All right, then let's get down to brass tacks." I leaned forward. "I don't know why you keep messing with me, Penny, but I'm sick of it. So consider this your official 'cease and desist' notice. Whatever you know, or *think* you know? I'm done making deals with you."

She watched me, stone-faced, and then turned her hand over in a "go on" gesture. "Is that all?"

"No, it's not." Heat bloomed across my chest, spreading up my neck. "This is the one and only time we're having a polite conversation, okay? If you don't drop this, there are still plenty of Serpents who want to settle old scores, and they're willing to rumble if I give the word."

"But you're not gonna do that. Are you, Jughead?" A feline smile toyed with one corner of her mouth. "Every time we've gone after it in the past, you've never fought your own battles by yourself. Always tattling to Mommy and Daddy, always rounding up your crew to keep the deck stacked in your favor. But here you are, all alone." She traced a groove in the table with her finger. "If you weren't worried about other people knowing what you're here for, you'd have already told your buddies and brought along backup. But you didn't."

I was simmering, the heat spreading into my face. "I came here alone as a courtesy. You've got no idea what kind of damage I can do one-on-one, though, so don't test me, *Poison Penny.*"

"Oh, we're name-calling now?" She scoffed. "Is that supposed to hurt my feelings or something? Your mother *gouged out my eye*, Jughead. Names don't bother me."

Annoyed by the act, I rapped the table. "Come off it. I'm just using the one you picked out for yourself—you know, in the letter you dropped on my doorstep this morning? *'I'm watching you'*?"

Penny's brow furrowed. "What the hell are you talking about?"

"You *know* what I'm talking about."

"A letter on your doorstep?" Her voice dripped with scorn. "You think if I wanted to get revenge on you and your family for all the hell you've put me through, I'd go all the way up to your front door and deliver a *letter*?" She made it sound so ridiculous that, for a moment, I started to doubt myself. "Take a look around, *Forsythe*. I'm not hanging out at this chemical toilet of a bar on a Sunday afternoon for my health. I actually work here, okay? I've been here all day, with Ajax, taking care of last night's receipts. I'm not your mailman."

"Maybe not." I wasn't going to just take her word for it, of course, but it didn't really matter. "You could've easily had one of your minions do it, though. One of the Ghoulies, or those Gargoyle freaks you were running with."

"Are you kidding me?" Penny barked an ugly laugh. "I don't have *minions*. You know what I've got—aside from an eye patch, a limp, and a scar on my arm that reminds me of the Jones family every single day?" Leaning into the light, she snarled, "I've got a law degree that's useless to me now, because I got suspended by the bar association for criminal activities. I've got this crummy dive and fourteen employees—thirteen, if our dishwasher is a no-show again, because it'll be his third strike—and that's *it*.

"The Serpents kicked me out, the Ghoulies are in the wind, and I was never part of the Gargoyles to begin with. Kurtz came to me because he knew I had an ax to grind, and he figured it wouldn't take much convincing to get me to tangle with Gladys in that asinine game you were playing." Slumping back, she added darkly, "And he was right. But these days, I've got no connections, Jones. No minions—just me."

The clock ticked as we sat there in an awkward silence—Penny brooding, and me digesting what she'd said. I still didn't trust her. She fit Poison Pen's profile to a tee . . . and even though this confession sounded truthful, it didn't mean she was innocent. There was no way to prove she'd really been at the Devil's Bargain all day, and Ajax would no doubt lie for her if I asked him. But with no leverage on my side to force the truth into the open, we were at an impasse.

Plus, a bunch of guys with tire irons were en route.

Getting to my feet, glaring daggers back down at Penny Peabody, I snapped, "This isn't over. Someone's coming after me, and if it turns out it's you, I'll make you regret it."

"Sounds nice, kid," she replied breezily. "If and when you ever figure out who's twisting your arm, tell them they can drink for free at the Devil's Bargain. For life."

Her hollow laughter followed me out of the bar and into the street.

As I walked, I analyzed her story, searching for lies—or for facts. The truth was that I was a little shaken by Penny's downfall. She'd always been a miserable character: a lying megalomaniac with no qualms about hurting people (unless the plan backfired). But I hadn't been prepared to find her reduced to these pitiful circumstances.

I was so lost in thought that I didn't see what was wrong with my bike until I was right in front of it. Until I saw the plain square envelope sitting on the leather seat—pinned into place with a kitchen knife.

CHAPTER TEN

Hi, Juggie!

Did you have fun chasing wild geese today? Sorry, but you're in the tall weeds out here—I don't even <u>like</u> Greendale. As soon as I leave this note, I'm out of this creepy place.

I have to admit, I got a little bit nervous earlier when I saw you with Archie at the Chock'Lit Shoppe—because I know how your mind works. You thought, "Here's another life-or-death situation, and I have to fix it," and you wanted to tell him. To warn him that Poison Pen was Out There and armed with dangerous information.

But you didn't, did you? This time, you decided to handle things on your own. It's funny . . . you've committed the Serpents to an awful lot of your personal battles. And you had Betty Cooper so involved with your intrigues at Stonewall that she put up a murder board in the office of the <u>Blue & Gold</u> so she could solve your problems for you in her spare time.

But when it came to this, when it came to a dirty little secret that threatens other people, you couldn't even tell your so-called best friend. Even though he's one of the ones who might get hit the hardest by the fallout. That's pretty cold, Jughead Jones.

But also pretty understandable. After all, you know what it means to suffer someone else's fallout. If you told Archie, he'd have gone into full Red Paladin mode, and we _both_ know what that means. Fists would have flown, heads would have rolled, and in the end? He'd have only made things worse for everyone.

I've decided on the price of my silence. Someone needs to tell Riverdale's redheaded vigilante exactly what a menace he is, and I want it to be you. High school is over, summer's ending, and nothing gold can stay . . . so let it go, Juggie. End your friendship with Archie Andrews—_for good_—and start the next phase of your life with a clean slate.

And do it today, in public, or I start telling people what I know. The former sheriff's son involved in a little GTA would make great copy on Rumordale.com, the _Register_, RIVW . . . and it would sure be a shame if that meant Sheriff Keller couldn't look the other way. For you <u>and</u> your accomplices. Lower the boom on Archie by midnight, or <u>I'll</u> make sure that you spend the next phase of your life behind bars.

I'll be watching.

—Poison Pen

∿∿∿

On the ride back to Riverdale, the sweat that rolled beneath my Serpents jacket, that gathered under my helmet and dripped down the back of my neck, was ice cold.

Penny Peabody hadn't pinned that note to my bike. There hadn't been enough time for her to write the message—in painstakingly squared-off letters, stripped of identifying characteristics—and still sneak in through the back. Not in the time it took me to disarm Ajax and lay him out on that disgusting floor. Even if she were faking the limp she said she'd gotten from when my mom put a Sai through her leg.

Ajax himself couldn't have done it, because I could see him behind the bar throughout our whole conversation—plus the wording alone exonerated him. A guy who didn't know what *precede* meant certainly didn't dash off a grammatically accurate threat letter (with a literary reference to *The Outsiders*, no less) in under five minutes.

My tires hummed as I rode back over the bridge and into Riverdale. If it wasn't Penny . . . who was it? Who knew me this well? *Who'd been there that night?* My lookout was innocent, I was sure of it, and that also went for the others who knew beforehand. But who did that leave?

The night of July Fourth flashed through my mind: the silent streets, the unlit windows. If someone saw me, recognized me—and hated me this much—why hadn't they used their knowledge before now?

Or maybe this new letter answered that question. After all, it was only a few weeks ago that the sheriff's office officially came under audit by the state. Before that, there were plenty of times that my friends and I had been cut slack by law enforcement when we were in trouble.

With an outside agency triple-checking Sheriff Keller's paperwork, and Deputy Huxley in the pocket of a gubernatorial candidate with Riverdale's crime rates in his campaign crosshairs, everything was different now. If the media really did start reporting on what I'd done, and Sheriff Keller tried to downplay it, he'd be turned into an example. And then so would I . . . along with everyone else who'd been part of what went down on July Fourth.

I was back on familiar streets before I knew it, sunlight flecking the pavement through the trees, and only when the sign for the Chock'Lit Shoppe came into view did I finally ask myself what might have been the most obvious question of all.

Out of everything Poison Pen could have made me do, holding my future over my head . . . why this? Instead of money or sex tapes or drug running, they wanted me to break up with my best friend. *Why?* Archie Andrews was one of the few constants from my whole messed-up childhood that I *didn't* want to say good-bye to. That I didn't lie awake in bed at night hoping I would live long enough to someday forget.

And Poison Pen made him the price I would have to pay to protect my secret, so I could keep everyone safe—me, my friends, and especially Archie himself.

Alone in the parking lot, the sun beating down on me and sweat dripping in my eyes, I read both letters over again. The ink was black, the handwriting boxy, and aside from the references to July Fourth, everything else mentioned was stuff anyone in Riverdale could have heard or read about in the news. I had enemies out there—malefactors I'd booted from the Serpents, grudge-bearing Ghoulies, Stonewall Preppers who hated me for the rot I'd revealed in their ivy-covered halls. It would take weeks to track and eliminate each suspect.

But I didn't have weeks. *"And do it today, in public, or I start telling people what I know."* I had one impossible choice: lose Archie's friendship . . . or lose everything.

The bell jingled overhead as I pushed my way back into the Chock'Lit Shoppe, midday light making the throwback chrome and vinyl look warm and inviting. My best friend was right where I'd left him, playfully arguing with Pop about some sports thing, and I walked to my old seat feeling simultaneously overheated and cold to the bone.

"Hey, you're back!" Archie's obvious delight at seeing me again made something twist sharply in my gut. "You get your laundry taken care of?"

It took me a moment to remember my excuse for leaving the diner so abruptly, and I mumbled a few words that sounded like an answer. Without missing a beat of their ongoing back-and-forth, Pop then started making me a milk shake to replace the one I'd abandoned, and I stared at the counter. Archie was resting his hand next to his now-empty plate, and the fresh scabs forming over his knuckles caught my eye.

"What happened to your fingers?" I blurted, interrupting their conversation.

"Huh?" Archie glanced at his injuries and his expression clouded. "Oh. There's this kid at the center who always shows up with these bruises on his face—or his neck, or his shoulders . . . you name it, he's had a fist-sized mark there. A couple of days ago, he finally told me it was his old man beating him up."

"Dear me." Pop looked seasick at the notion. "That poor child. Whoever could do such a thing?"

"And you . . . dealt with it," I supplied tonelessly.

"I know his dad. Sort of." Archie flexed his swollen hand. "He worked a job for Andrews Construction back in December but he wasn't reliable, and we ended up letting him go. I wish

I'd known then that . . . anyway, yeah. I went down there to confront him, and tell him to leave his son alone."

The milk shake appeared in front of me, water rolling down the sides of the glass. "And he didn't like that, so, naturally, you ended up whaling on the guy."

"He took a swing at me," Archie confirmed, but he was looking at me funny. "Is something the matter, Jug?"

"Nope. What would be the matter?" I could feel Poison Pen's corkscrew eyes, coming from every corner of the room at once. "Hey, did you think of calling the cops first?"

"Why?" He turned on his stool to face me a little more squarely, that funny look getting a little darker. "So they could issue a warning—make him even more pissed off—and then walk away without actually doing anything? No, I didn't call them."

"You don't think he's angrier *now*?" In spite of everything, I could have laughed at the absurdity. "What about Child Protective Services, or one of those social workers who are down at the center all the time, talking to those kids? You call one of them?"

"No, Jug, I didn't." His whole body had gone still. "Because *Ms. Weiss* wasn't gonna clean this guy's clock—and, trust me, that's the only language these animals understand." With a minute jerk of his chin, he prompted, "Listen, if there's something you want to say, then just say it."

"It never ends with you, does it, Archie?" I could feel the

snowball gathering speed and mass, rolling downhill. Every part of me wanted to stop it, but instead I just stepped out of its way. "What happens if the only lesson you taught this guy is that his kid ratted him out? What if he learned that he has an enemy at the community center, and the only way to beat him is to bring backup? Or a weapon?"

"Then I'll deal with it," Archie shot back. "It wouldn't be the first time, you know."

"No! Of *course* I know—that's the point!" Shoving my milk shake away, I turned on him. "That's your *pattern*, Archie Andrews. You're a hammer, and the whole world looks like a nail to you! You solve every problem with your fists, and it always blows up in your face. *Always*."

"You didn't mind my problem-solving techniques the night Penelope Blossom made me fight that eight-foot-tall Viking to keep us all alive," he pointed out hotly.

"And you're not the only one who gets hit by the shrapnel, either." I barged ahead, hands tingling. "How many innocent people did Hiram Lodge hurt because of your two-man grudge match? How many of your friends were collateral in your war with Dodger Dickenson? You opened the community center to help disadvantaged kids, and then you almost got them all killed on Thanksgiving!" Shoving myself up from the counter, heat throbbing at my temples, I finally blurted something I'd been trying not to say for months. "*You got my dad shot, Archie!* Here! Right here, at the only place in

Riverdale that has still felt like home to me since the Twilight closed!"

There was a dead silence in the diner, and I finally realized I'd been shouting—that every single eye in the room really was on me after all. Archie was pale, a storm of emotions staging a clear battle in his expression. Finally, he let out a heavy breath. "Jug . . ."

"Don't say you're sorry." I thrust my hands out. "It's too late—and you'd do everything the same all over again if you had the chance, because that's who you are." Snatching up my things, I started for the door, my chest tight as a vise. "You've got a hero complex, Archie, and you're going to destroy everyone you know trying to save them. Just look at what's happening because—"

And I froze, blinking hard—because I couldn't finish that thought out loud. *Just look at what's happening because of July Fourth.* What twisted irony.

Getting to his feet, running a hand through his ginger hair, Archie began, "Jug, listen. I know I didn't man up and say something to you when your dad got hurt, and that's—"

"Stop, just *stop*." Words were getting harder to say, my vision marbled by unshed tears. "I have to go. Don't follow me, and . . . and don't call."

Slamming through the door and out into the parking lot, choking on the thick, humid air, my lungs hitched. Somewhere behind me, Archie was sitting with the weight of my accusations—a mix of honest anger and falsified outrage—and trying to make sense of it. I hoped that someday I'd be able to explain myself. To fix things before it was too late.

I had to hope that Poison Pen was satisfied.

Slinging a leg over my bike, kicking it into gear, I roared away from the Chock'Lit Shoppe, pouring on speed until the trees became a blur and the curving road a dangerous dance on two wheels. The tires whined, and the wind tore at my clothes, and I bit down until my jaw throbbed.

Riverdale had won again.

∧∧∧

Unknown ID:

Good boy! You should've seen the look on Archie's face when you finished him. It was a masterstroke, Juggie. My compliments.

Jughead:

This isn't over. I'm going to figure out who you are.

Unkown ID:

And then what?

Jughead:

Archie isn't the only one who can settle problems with violence.

Careful . . . remember how many people I can bury with the dirt I've got! And you know what they say—if you go seeking revenge, first you'd better dig two graves . . .

Jughead:

It'll be a pleasure.

[ERROR—MESSAGE UNDELIVERABLE]

I have to admit, that one was satisfying. Getting Jughead Jones to accuse Archie Andrews of imperiling others? As if Jughead's little Gone Girl act didn't make his three best friends the most hated and feared kids in Riverdale. As if the Chock'Lit Shoppe—and everyone in it—was never besieged by out-of-control Ghoulies looking for revenge on the Serpent King.

The fact is, they're both guilty. Neither of them thinks more than a single step ahead. Neither of them has ever spared a thought for who else gets drowned by the undertow of their actions—but I'm going to change that.

Jughead was absolutely right about Archie's need to play the hero, but what our little brooding Southside philosopher failed to admit is that he has a rather compulsive need to play the crusading victim of forces beyond his control, conspiracies. One has a hero complex, and the other has a persecution complex, but what Archie and Jughead have in common is that they both need to be the center of attention.

To lay all my cards on the table, though? I did worry just a little bit about the trouble I might expect from Jughead Jones. Not because I thought he'd resist my orders . . . but because he never met a mystery that he didn't try to solve.

And there's still a lot to accomplish before I can let him catch up to me. I've got a list of names, and only two have been scratched off, so I need to get busy.

See, Jughead isn't the only boy in town with a penchant for melodrama. There are plenty of other attention-starved actors crowding this particular stage . . . and unfortunately for them, I'm the one manning the spotlight.

And I think I've chosen my new star . . .

—Poison Pen

PART THREE
KEVIN KELLER
MONDAY

CHAPTER ELEVEN

Hey stranger! Congrats on that rave review for your Saturday night gig!

Josie:

Kev! Omg you saw that? Isn't it wild?

Kevin:

A professional critic wrote "Clear the Top 40 and get out of Josie McCoy's way." Your mother sent it to literally everyone in her contacts.

Josie:

SHE is who the Top 40 should be scared of. If they don't go willingly, Sierra McCoy will clear that list with her bare hands lol

Josie:

Anyway, the gig went great, but honestly the best part was just performing in a REAL VENUE in a REAL CITY. Not that I'm dragging La Bonne Nuit or Riverdale, but . . .

Kevin:

Oh, no, please. Drag away! In fact, I would LOVE if you would just drag Riverdale all the way into the ocean? I have had pretty much all the quaint small-town charm I can survive.

Josie:

Just breathe, babe. In a week, you'll be leaving it all in your rearview.

Kevin:

Not a week—eight entire days. 192 hours, and I am counting them down to the minute I get to leave. Riverdale has been . . . particularly Riverdale while you've been on your tour.

Josie:

I actually have no idea if that means "boring" or if that means "corpses are piling up again."

Kevin:

The fact that it could mean either is exactly why I cannot wait for my college experience to begin. Pittsburgh! Carnegie Mellon! Pretending to be a young Andy Warhol! Living my Logan-Lerman-in-Perks-of-Being-a-Wallflower fantasy!

Josie:

Dating prospects beyond just the four gay guys in Riverdale, most of whom are either on their way to jail or just getting back out!

Kevin:

OUCH. But . . . yes.

Josie:

I hadn't wanted to pry, but . . . does this mean your on-again-off-again with Mr. Fangs Fogarty is currently off?

Kevin:

We are . . . on hiatus. Riverdale is too cursed for dating, so we agreed to be Single for the Summer, and start fresh in the fall. A blank slate, if you will.

Josie:

Nothing wrong with that. And in the meantime?

Kevin:

Who knows? A temporary fling? I might even meet a guy I can bond with over something other than how we both got brainwashed by a cult leader and had our kidneys stolen.

#RelationshipGoals

⌒⌒⌒

Someone on our block was mowing their lawn, and the incessant roar of the blades was absolutely ruining the experience of my fifth listen to the original Broadway cast recording of *Dear Evan Hansen*—that day. It had also ruined my fourth listen, and part of the third as well. The album runs for about an hour, and the lawns in our neighborhood aren't even that big, so I have *no* idea what was going on out there.

It was also about nine thousand degrees in my room, the air as dense and wet as boiled oatmeal—but according to my dad, *"Air-conditioning is too expensive, and unless you're planning to pay for it yourself, you've got a window that opens just fine."* So I was lying on my bed with the window open, my ceiling fan stirring hot oatmeal around, while the neighbor's lawn mower drowned out every one of Laura Dreyfuss's high notes.

I could, of course, have chosen to listen to it with my earbuds, or with the expensive headphones Ronnie gave me for Christmas last year, *but that is not how Broadway is meant to be experienced*. I mean, it is practically already a crime that I had to hear all these songs for the first time from a *recording* and not from sitting in the audience at the Music Box. Musical theater must fill the entire performance space—literally, every single molecule of air all the way up to the rafters ringing with gorgeous, emotive song—and you're not getting that from *earbuds*.

But it's not like I'm rolling around in opportunities to take in Broadway's hottest shows. This is *Riverdale*. What can really be said for a town where the most sophisticated, au courant theater being performed within a fifty-mile radius is at the local high school?

The casual observer might wonder who on earth listens to the same original Broadway cast recording for five hours straight on a Monday afternoon—and the answer, for the record, would be *"people who are depressed."*

For my whole life, I've bemoaned the Riverdaleness of my existence. Growing up gay in a town known for maple syrup and murder, where there are more people in cult deprogramming than in the local chapter of PFLAG (and okay, yes, there's a considerable amount of overlap), has been hard. My ex-boyfriends include: a gang member who went to prison for helping to cover up a murder, now dead from cyanide poisoning; a closeted athlete, who left town after his father kidnapped and terrorized us; and then Fangs, another gang member—who was falsely accused of murder, got shot, sold drugs, killed somebody for real, joined a cult (with me, it must be said), lost a kidney, *stayed* in the cult, and then . . . okay, helped me make tickle videos after that.

Do not ask about tickle videos. Some of life's avenues are too dark to revisit.

Now, I know it's unhealthy to base your notion of happiness on romance. In fact, no one in Riverdale knows that as well as I do. My longest relationship was probably Joaquin (gang member, juvie, cyanide) unless you count all the times I hooked up with Moose (athlete, closeted, homophobic dad) before we were official. But I don't, because Moose was more committed to his on-again-off-again girlfriend, Midge (deceased), back then, and wouldn't even kiss me for *months*. Even when they were off-again!

My point is, I've had plenty of time to be single, to enjoy being a friend (and then a third wheel, and then a fifth wheel), but I've never had an actual healthy romantic relationship of my own. Joaquin only pursued me because I was the sheriff's son and the Serpents wanted intel on the Jason Blossom investigation. Moose took advantage of me when he didn't have Midge, and then he split town right when we had a chance to become something *real*.

And Fangs . . . well, murder, drugs, cult, lies, tickle videos. (We were talking about a fresh start in Pittsburgh in the fall, but with a history of nothing but romantic disasters, I couldn't take anything for granted.) Bottom line: For the first time in my life, I just wanted a shot at what my straight friends already had—a dating pool, a community of peers who knew what I'm going through, an opportunity to be myself and chase my dreams and maybe not have to do it alone.

But. Despite my countdown clock, despite my Broadway

ambitions, and despite all the pain and misery and messed-up things I'd endured here . . . the thought of leaving Riverdale was somehow also scary? I had a burger at Pop's last week, and the fries were burned, and I started to tear up, because I didn't know when I'd eat burned fries at Pop's again. I've never lived anywhere but Riverdale, and leaving—even if I can't wait to do it (one hundred and ninety hours and thirty-four minutes to go!)—kind of means changing who I think I am.

So I was depressed, and I was listening to *Dear Evan Hansen*, and I was maybe relating more to all the angst than I should have.

There was a sudden explosive *chunk-a-chunk* sound then, as the neighbor's lawn mower found a hidden rock and choked to death on it. The blades ground to a halt, and an anguished cry sounded—followed by a torrent of unrepeatable words. Against the relative silence, Laura Dreyfuss belted out her high notes in "Only Us," and I felt my whole body relax. Every now and then, even in Riverdale, things could still come up Kevin.

This, of course, was the exact moment a huge fist pounded at my bedroom door. "Kev? It's me. Can I come in?"

My dad. While I have lots of reason to complain about Stuff My Parents Do, respecting my privacy was one of the things they scrupulously did right. "Sure."

I turned off the music just as the door opened, Dad poking his head in like a groundhog trying not to see its shadow. "Sorry for interrupting. I know I'm supposed to be at work, but my damn cell battery died, and I forgot to bring a charger to the station. There was a letter for you in the mailbox."

"A letter? Like snail mail?" I wrinkled my nose, trying to remember the last time I got something in a physical envelope that wasn't a debit card or a passive-aggressive note from a texting-resistant grandparent wondering why they hadn't "heard" from me. "Who is it from?"

"I don't know, there's no return address." Dad frowned at the envelope he was holding. "No stamp, either. Must've been hand-delivered."

"How mysterious." I sat up, intrigued. "And how gratifyingly theatrical!"

"If you say so." One corner of my dad's mouth quirked up in a smile, and he tossed me the envelope—a plain white square. "Seems like a lot of trouble when the cost of a stamp will get you door-to-door service from the USPS."

"It's about presentation, Dad," I explained, exasperated. "Where's the romance in a postage stamp?"

"Ask Elizabeth Barrett Browning." He was oh so smug.

Fact: In 1844, poet Elizabeth Barrett gained the attention and admiration of fellow poet Robert Browning—six years her junior. The pair began a clandestine correspondence via the mail, fell madly in love, and married against her father's vehement wishes. She died young, of course, because she understood the value of theatricality.

Dad only knows about Elizabeth Barrett Browning because

Sonnets from the Portuguese is one of Sierra's favorite collections of love poetry, and he uses his knowledge as a bludgeon whenever possible.

He was leaning against my doorframe, his sheriff's uniform looking like he'd slept in it. Although the dark circles under his eyes suggested he maybe hadn't slept at all. "Everything okay, Dad? You look a little . . ."

"Haggard? Frazzled? On the verge of a stress blackout?"

Considering, I answered, "D—all the above."

He mustered a rueful smile. "You know, for the first few months after I was forced to resign, I wanted my job back so badly I could taste it. And now that I've been reinstated . . ."

"Be careful what you wish for?"

"Something like that." Sighing, he said, "Ever since that fiasco at the Five Seasons over the weekend, Patrick Pendergast has been making my life a living hell. Whoever tampered with that slideshow . . . it wasn't technically illegal, but he's decided it's more evidence of how badly local law enforcement is failing the county."

"To be fair, your first replacement was a stooge for Hiram Lodge," I noted lightly, reminding him of Sheriff Minetta's brief (and undeniably corrupt) tenure.

"Yeah, well. I'm not saying he doesn't have something of a point." Dad smirked a little. "But the pressure he's putting on us—and on the mayor, and on the board of county supervisors— is only interfering with our operations. He's built his whole campaign for governor around being 'tough on crime,' and it's no secret Riverdale has . . . let's just say, unusually high statistics in that area. Pendergast's opponent is really hammering him in the ads for failing to keep order in his own district."

"And so he's been hammering you."

"He's the one who insisted on this good-for-nothing audit that's hamstringing my entire force!" Dad rubbed his face wearily. "I can't even order paper clips without having the forms examined by three different outside observers who answer to three different masters."

For months, Pendergast had been smack-talking Riverdale's municipal government, criticizing the sheriff's office and the mayor for their handling of our town's "unusually high" crime statistics. After a mugging sent one of his volunteers to the hospital with a switchblade in his gut—an ugly case, in which misleading evidence almost landed the wrong person behind bars—the senator took off his metaphorical gloves. Currently, the Rockland County Sheriff's Office was being subjected to an audit, a full review of its policies, procedures, and personnel, to determine whether they were doing the job right.

"And now that Huxley is marrying into the family, Pendergast basically has a spy in my station house to report back anything he thinks the auditors won't." His eyes darkened, his focus on something a long way off—which was frankly a relief, because it meant he didn't notice me going rigid at the change in subject. "If I could figure out a way to let that little glory-hounding twerp go, I would. He and his partner made that bad arrest back in June—they hurt that kid! The family could've sued the office, if they'd had a mind to."

This wasn't news to me, but I kept my face carefully blank. Sweat gathered at the small of my back as I tried to think of how to redirect the conversation without being obvious about it. "Maybe you'll get lucky and the auditors will catch him stealing office supplies."

My dad suppressed a grin. "I'm not that lucky."

Finally, he gave a good-bye salute and retreated from the room, leaving me and my haywire heartbeat to calm down in peace. Reflexively, I looked at the clock. One hundred and ninety hours and twenty minutes to go until I could escape conversations that brushed up against panic-inducing subject matter. Fanning myself with the envelope to dry the moisture at my temples, I began reciting the Tony Award–winning musicals in reverse chronological order to de-stress myself.

The envelope I was holding was a perfect square—symmetrically pleasing—and it was sealed with a circle of red wax. I fought back goose bumps. Truly, the math involved was clear: hand-delivered mail, quality paper stock, the vintage flourish of a *wax seal* with an inscrutable monogram ("PP"?). I mean, obviously this was some new enterprise by Cheryl Blossom and/or Veronica Lodge. No one else in this town would have the nerve.

Eagerly, I broke the seal and opened the flap, and as I fished out the letter folded inside, three photographs came with it, tumbling onto my bed. One landed faceup, and when I realized what I was looking at, time slowed down, my heart sped up again, and I felt the blood drain from my face.

It was me, my back against a brick wall at night, artfully framed by a cone of stark light cast down by an overhead lamp. And I was making out, *very aggressively*, with one Deputy Hayes Huxley.

∧∧∧

Dear Kevin,

How does it feel to be Riverdale's resident sidekick? Everybody's favorite also-ran—not as smart as Betty or as popular as Veronica; not as loved as Archie or as feared as Cheryl; not as complex as Jughead, as charming as Reggie, or as brave as Toni. Actually, Kevvie, you'll have to remind me . . . what <u>do</u> you bring to the table?

You introduced acts at La Bonne Nuit—a job that could be managed by a chalkboard—and aside from the occasional bon mot, what else have you accomplished in your time at Riverdale High? Your first attempt at mounting a musical spectacular was derailed by a serial killer, your second doubled as a recruitment drive for a nefarious brainwasher, and your third got shut down by Principal Honey before it even reached the stage. How many of your classmates did you talk into having their organs harvested, anyway? They all let you hang out with them, but maybe that's just because you make them feel better about themselves by comparison.

Here is where I'd ordinarily start in on your sad excuse for a love life, but . . . I believe the enclosed pictures speak for themselves.

On the night of July Fourth, you played tonsil hockey with Hayes Huxley out back of the Rockland County Sheriff's Office, while his fiancée sat at home, alone. (Tell me, and please be honest, did the deputy at least invite you to his fabulous engagement party at the Five Seasons last Saturday?)

Cheaters never win, Kevin, and while Deputy Huxley has quite a bit to lose if this gets out . . . so do you. See, I know exactly what led up to this furtive little clinch, as well as what dominoes would start to fall if the whole truth were to be revealed.

And I'm talking the <u>whole</u> truth. You know what I mean.

Lucky for you, I am capable of showing compassion. Sometime very soon, I'm going to ask you to perform a certain task—and if you cooperate, no one will ever have to know what was really going on that night. If you don't? Well, then it's every man for himself.

In the meantime, the price of my mercy is your silence. If you tell anyone about me or this letter, your secrets will spread through town faster than Fizzle Rocks, and I promise you I <u>will</u> know if you cross me. Loose lips sink ships, my dear, and yours doesn't look particularly seaworthy . . .

I'll be watching.

—Poison Pen

CHAPTER TWELVE

My vision tunneled, the room spun like a carousel, and the pictures became somehow louder than the neighbor's lawn mower. It felt like the whole neighborhood could see the photos as I fumbled them back into the envelope and squeezed the flap shut with trembling hands. For a moment, I tried to will the whole thing away, to tell myself it was too preposterous to be real—but, this being Riverdale, I knew my denial was wasted energy.

Someone knew.

Not only knew, but could prove it. My future flashed before my eyes—a split-screen Choose Your Own Adventure, where one path led to Broadway (via Pittsburgh), and the other to shame, disgrace . . . and possible prison time. My heart dropped through the floor. I liked a bad boy as much as anyone (and have certainly dated more than my share), but I was absolutely not cut out for life behind bars.

In that moment, I knew I had no choice. The plain fact of it was, I really did have a lot to lose—and others had even more. *Numerous* futures would be upended, destroyed, if the whole story of my liaison with Deputy Huxley became public knowledge. Somehow my friends had forgiven me for what I'd done to them out of fealty to Edgar Evernever. And now I could be the one to cost them everything? After all the work I'd done to regain their trust?

Reopening the envelope, I stared at the photos and read the letter a few more times. *"I know exactly what led up to this furtive little clinch . . . I'm talking the* whole *truth."*

It couldn't be possible, but pictures don't lie.

Someone had been there. Someone really knew about July Fourth.

⌃⌃⌃

Independence Day in Riverdale was a signature blend of hokey traditions and legitimately fun activities—even if I would not be caught dead admitting such out loud. The parade, the pie contest, the dunk tank, and the fireworks display? I'd spent my whole life looking forward to those events each year.

But this summer, on the evening of July Fourth, I had only one thing on my mind: Hayes Huxley.

To be clear, I knew exactly four things about Deputy Huxley: (1) He had graduated from Riverdale High the same year as Betty's sister, Polly; (2) he had thick, dark hair and heavy eyebrows (which . . . let's face it, is kind of exactly my type); (3) he'd joined the sheriff's office after my dad had been forced to resign his post, making him something of an enigma to me; and (4) back before the Black Hood's reign of terror put me off cruising for good, I had hooked up with Hayes more than once out in Fox Forest.

For those who went seeking companionship in the woods at night, anonymity was often part of the appeal. Lots of guys live or work in environments where they don't feel safe being open about their sexuality, and clandestine assignations on Riverdale's wooded hillsides offered a certain freedom. Back then, when he was just someone I made out with now and then by the light of the moon, the notion he might be hiding something . . . didn't seem so shocking.

And then I quit cruising, and Hayes Huxley's square jaw, soft lips, and dark hair gradually faded from my mind. I didn't think I'd see him again.

So, when I found myself on the sidewalk outside the sheriff's station on July Fourth, staring through the broad front window at a familiar, boldly eyebrowed face behind the front desk, I didn't know that he was in a relationship. I *definitely* didn't know that he was *engaged*—to the daughter of a state senator, no less. All I knew was that if I wanted to go in there and talk to him, I needed a better icebreaker than "Hey, remember the time we stepped in a pile of fire ants while making out against a maple tree?"

As I stood there, workshopping casual introductions, two men emerged from the station and headed for a patrol car at the curb. One of them was Deputy Carlson, who'd joined under my dad's first tenure in office; and as he and his partner drove off, I knew I'd finally run out of time to indulge my self-doubt. Screwing my courage to the sticking place, I took a deep breath and headed inside.

Deputy Huxley glanced up from his computer screen, and his expression underwent a series of rapid shifts. He recognized me, I could tell . . . but was he happy about it? Darting a glance around the empty room, he leaned back in his chair. Then, smooth as silk, he asked, "Is there something I can help you with, sir?"

"You know, I think maybe there is." I gave him my most killer smile, the one I always used to tease Moose, back when he wanted to pretend there was nothing between us. "I recently recognized someone I haven't seen for a long time, and I'm trying to figure out if he remembers me as fondly as I remember him."

Tenting his fingers under his chin, Huxley affected a pensive frown—but I saw the glint in his eye. "I'm not sure that's something the sheriff's office can help you with."

"Really? Maybe it would help if I described him. He's very handsome." I couldn't believe this cool, suave voice was coming out of me—me! My flesh pebbled all over just hearing it.

Flirting is amazing and terrifying.

A cocky smirk pulled at Huxley's lips. "Is that so?"

"Mm-hm. Dark hair, dark eyes, perfect lips . . . that's what I remember most about him. He was a very, very good kisser."

"Interesting detail. That could be helpful," Huxley murmured, his eyes tracing the shape of my mouth—but he was still playing it cool. "It could be this friend of yours remembers you, too. How did you happen to find him again?"

"It's the funniest thing." I'm decidedly more of a director than a performer, but I was quite proud of the Wide-Eyed Innocent act I affected just then. "I was on my way to my car, and I noticed him through a window. I would have kept walking, but . . . well, as I believe I mentioned, he was a very, *very* good kisser." I smiled again. "Maybe it was a coincidence, or maybe it was fate, but I got really curious to see if he remembers me, too."

There was a loaded silence, the air around us fizzing with electricity, and I watched Deputy Huxley's eyes go dark and hungry. Rising from his chair, he stated, in a low voice, "I'm the only one here right now, so I can't be away from my desk for very long."

"That's okay." I was practically purring. "I'll take what I can get."

I reached for his collar, but he deflected my hand, shooting a warning glance at the front window. "Not here. Follow me."

Under other circumstances, I might have been insulted by the rebuff, but it suited me just fine for us to get reacquainted in private. I figured he was closeted at work, or afraid it would be unprofessional to suck face with a relative stranger while on duty. Regardless, I offered no resistance when he took my hand and led me along a short warren of hallways, guiding me through a metal door and into an alley running alongside the station house.

We were barely outside before he shoved me against the rough brick wall and pressed those perfect lips against my own. Perhaps I'd been laying it on a bit thick when I was flirting, but Hayes Huxley really was a phenomenal kisser. Within seconds, I'd blown a few circuits in my brain. To tell the absolute truth, I forgot what I was doing out there—my awareness limited to mouths and hands and warm, huffing breath. We might have been lip-locked for five minutes or ten, maybe even fifteen, when he finally pulled back.

His pupils were wide and dilated, one calloused hand buried in my hair, and he rasped, "I'd love to continue this later. What are you—"

But that's as far as he got, because at that exact moment, the metal door exploded open again. A figure in a leather jacket—and a terrifyingly familiar black hood—burst out of the station house, took one look at Huxley and me, and then set off at a dead sprint for the mouth of the alley.

Huxley shouted, giving chase—but I was already running like hell in the opposite direction. I made it halfway to Pickens Park before I realized the explosions I'd heard were gunshots and not fireworks.

⌃⌃⌃

The thing about receiving a scary note that threatens to unravel your entire life and also warns you not to tell is that you have to act normal afterward. It was my second-to-last Monday left in Riverdale, and I had planned a farewell tour: eight days of antics, to be kicked off by ice cream sundaes downtown with Betty. All I wanted to do was cancel on her and lean into a panic attack . . . but I couldn't. Not only would it be difficult to come up with an unsuspicious last-minute excuse, but maybe meeting with her would help me identify "Poison Pen."

Not that I was going to ask Betty. *"I'll be watching"* was a rather pedestrian threat, but the inclusion of high-resolution photographs showing me tongue-wrestling with Senator Pendergast's future son-in-law gave it some considerable credence. Whoever this person was, they really did have eyes on me. Just thinking about it sent my heart lurching into my throat again, and I recited musicals all the way back to *Ain't Misbehavin'* (1978) before I gave up on trying to settle my nerves.

Still, I scrubbed the clammy sweat off my palms, threw on a clean shirt, and marched out the front door just the same. I took that Junior FBI training course under Betty's creepy/hot half brother, Charles, and I'd learned a few things; if someone was following me, maybe I could spot *them*, too.

ᴧᴧᴧ

As it so happened, spotting a tail is apparently much easier for TV detectives than for future Broadway directors. I drove at a snail's pace, my eyes on the rearview mirror more than they were on the road—until I nearly plowed over a mailbox. But without turning all the way around in my seat, it was impossible to see more than a few cars behind me. Eventually I had to just give up.

"I'll be watching." The hair on the back of my neck stood all the way up and danced. Until everything went to hell at the end, there was no one in that alley but me and Huxley, I was certain. I mean, I would absolutely have noticed a photographer snapping pictures. But the photos Poison Pen sent me were high quality, shot at ground level. The only rational explanation was that someone with a sophisticated camera had been positioned at the end of the passage, using a long-range lens so as to not be seen.

The question I was avoiding the hardest, the one that really made my brain melt, was *why me*? Who could have followed me, who could have possibly known where I would be that night or what I would be doing?

Chills rocketed up my spine as it occurred to me, for the first time, that only a select number of people *had* known exactly what I'd be doing that night. *They* were the most likely suspects, if I was looking for someone who could have arranged for me to be photographed in flagrante delicto. For a terrible moment, I choked on some dark suspicions about the people I trusted most in Riverdale.

Then, deliberately, I shoved the thought away. I refused to even consider it, unless and until I had no other choice. Everyone with foreknowledge of my actions on July Fourth had as much to lose as I did (or more), if truths were told. We'd sworn an oath of secrecy, and I couldn't imagine any of them breaking it—and certainly not to torment me.

But that was maybe the worst part. Whoever Poison Pen was, however they knew *"exactly what led up to this furtive little clinch,"* they'd gotten their hands on something that could destroy my friends. All thanks to me.

For some reason, someone had been lying in wait to catch me with my tongue in Pernilla Pendergast's fiancé's mouth, and I'd just blundered into a perfectly posed photo for them. And now . . . all those dominoes Poison Pen promised to topple were poised to land on people I cared about.

The zombie apocalypse disaster movie that is my love life had struck again.

∿∿∿

Betty was waiting for me at Jordan's Creamery, a little boutique ice cream shop about six blocks from the FBI field office where we'd studied how serial killers think. I was tempted to barge back into that ill-lit basement and beg someone to analyze my mail, but instead, I sat with Betty, poking my spork into a strawberry sundae while she filled me in on the latest of her mother's separation-anxiety-fueled breakdowns.

"Every morning this week, I've woken up to the sound of her sobbing into a throw pillow just outside my bedroom door." Betty downed a mouthful of hot fudge like it was revenge.

"A throw pillow?"

"It's a *special* throw pillow. Some great-aunt I've never even heard of embroidered it for me when I was born—it's got, like, a clown with a fishing pole on it. *A clown.* I mean, apparently that serial killer gene goes way back." She gripped her forehead. "Anyway, Mom hid it in the attic for eighteen years because it's *terrifying,* but now it's 'all she has left of my childhood' and she won't put it down. The other day, I woke up to find her literally *hovering over me, holding the clown pillow and sobbing.* I seriously thought it was the end."

"Mm-hmm." I made a frowny face, because her tone called for it. "The end."

Betty licked some more hot fudge off her spork and examined me. "Kevin, is everything okay?"

"Huh? Oh, yeah!" I stirred my sundae more vigorously, to show how much energy I had. "Yeah, things are great. College, here I come! One hundred and eighty-nine hours to go! Give or take."

"Okay." She nodded a little, ponytail swinging like Edgar Allan Poe's pendulum. "Because you haven't actually listened to a thing I've said since we sat down, and if you churn that ice cream any more it'll turn into butter."

"I like butter," I retorted—but she was right, and I pushed the sundae away from me. There was a lot I couldn't say, but I had to say *something*; and while Poison Pen had been unnecessarily cruel, the letter got at least one thing right. I was not as smart as Betty. "I've been . . . feeling guilty. About something that I did on July Fourth."

She flinched, as I expected she might, and before I could say anything else, she darted forward. "Kevin—"

"I know, I know, the first rule of July Fourth is don't talk about July Fourth," I whispered back in a rush, "and I'm not! I'm only talking about . . . what I did. On July Fourth."

Her body language remained tense—and, believe me, I got it. Mine was, too. We were seated outside, because the air-conditioned *inside* was packed, and I could *feel* the telephoto lens taking pictures from whatever angle I was facing at any given moment.

"I made out with a guy who was cheating on his fiancée!" I exclaimed as quietly as possible. "I was the Other Man—the *side piece*. I had to smile and nod through my dad's entire blow-by-blow of that engagement party, and the whole time, all I could think about was how Sierra called me out last month because of the *hickey* Hayes gave me!"

"Kevin." Betty reached across and grabbed my hands, holding them steady. "Listen to me. You're not the one who did anything wrong. Not really." I started to protest, but she cut me off. "Did you know he was engaged? Did you know he was even seeing someone at all?"

"No," I admitted—although it was not entirely the point. "Believe it or not, his personal life didn't actually come up."

I found out a week later, along with everybody else, when Pernilla Pendergast casually dropped the name of her fiancé in an email to Veronica. *That* was a lively group chat between those of us who knew *"exactly what led up to this furtive little clinch."*

"Then you're not the one who's at fault here. *He* made a commitment to somebody else, and it's his responsibility to honor it; if you didn't know, and he didn't tell you, then . . . Kev, I hate to say it, but he used you."

Her tone was reassuring, but a cold thing shifted under my skin all the same.

What happens in Fox Forest, stays in Fox Forest. It was a handy axiom I'd repeated to myself on occasion while cruising, when I'd run into someone I knew wasn't out yet. A couple of Ghoulies, a guy from Centerville High's soccer team, the cute nerd who ran Riverdale's abstinence club because his dad made him. A lot of don't ask, don't tell happened in the woods—it was mutual protection. We shared what felt safe, and we held back what didn't.

For example, I definitely didn't broadcast that I was the sheriff's son.

The times I encountered Hayes Huxley, I didn't exactly make him fill out a questionnaire before we got down to business under the maple trees. So, for all I know, he was dating Pernilla Pendergast even way back then—it had never occurred to me to ask. In a sense, we'd used each other.

"I'm not sure that's true," I muttered, watching strawberry syrup and vanilla ice cream swirl into a mushy pink soup. "I went in there that night because I wanted him to kiss me. We didn't run into each other by accident, and he didn't seek me out and lie to me—I pursued him. He wouldn't have cheated if I hadn't . . . seduced him."

"You are gorgeous and charming, but you're also giving yourself way too much credit." Betty offered me an affectionately cockeyed smile. "You didn't hypnotize him . . . all you did was present an opportunity. He could've said no. He didn't, and that's on him."

"But my motives weren't exactly pure, were they?" This kernel of guilt lay at the bottom of it all, like "The Princess and the Pea": a teeny source of discomfort that kept getting worse the more I focused on it. "I manipulated him, Betty, even if it wasn't by forcing him into something against his will." Looking her in the eye, I asked, "If I *had* known about Pernilla . . . would it have changed what we did that night?"

She was still trying to come up with an answer when my phone buzzed with an incoming message.

Unknown ID:

I scream, you scream, we all scream with BOREDOM. You and Betty have your heads awfully close together, Kev, but I'm glad to hear you've kept my letter a secret. Your guilt over playing kissy-face with the duplicitous deputy, however, is quite precious, I must say— especially given what else you and your friends have done.

Time to face facts, Lips Ahoy. Uninspired platitudes from a serial killer's daughter are not going to help you alleviate your shame—TRUTH is what's good for the soul. So here's your task: Tell Pernilla Pendergast what her fiancé is up to behind her back, and do it today. In person.

If you don't . . . well, I'll start telling some truths on your behalf. Like what brought you into the station house on July Fourth in the first place. And who interrupted you and Hot Lips Huxley in the alley. Beat me to the punch, lover—you have until 8:00 p.m. Tick tock . . .

CHAPTER THIRTEEN

Shooting up from my seat, I spun in a tight circle, chills racing up my spine. There were people everywhere—filling the courtyard, lingering in the parking lot, crowding the tiny creamery—and the whole time we'd been sitting there, customers had walked back and forth near our table. But no one was watching now. *Who had overheard us?*

"Kevin?" Betty's eyes were so wide I could see the whites all the way around her pale irises. "What is it—what's wrong?"

"It's . . ." Nerves made my stomach cramp. "I don't feel good! I . . . need to go home."

"But—"

"I'm sorry, Betty. I'll call you tomorrow!" I didn't wait for her to answer. Turning on my heel, I stumbled crookedly for the sidewalk and took off in a panicked jog, heading for my car. I'd parked four blocks away, and the sun beat down like a hammer, the air too thick to breathe.

Every person I passed became a suspect, every dark window a vantage point for a spy with a long-range lens. *Or a parabolic microphone?* Maybe Poison Pen could listen in from afar just as easily as they could take photos. I definitely had made the right choice by keeping my mouth shut, but what was I supposed to do *now*?

"Tell Pernilla Pendergast what her fiancé is up to behind her back." Thinking about it made me woozy with fear, and I had to bend over, sucking thick, warm air into my lungs. I could imagine it the way you can imagine falling off a skyscraper or getting eaten by a shark, ice-cold fingers wrapping themselves around my intestinal tract and squeezing.

Hello, Ms. Pendergast, my name is Kevin Keller, and I know what your fiancé's ChapStick tastes like! An inappropriate laugh sprang to my lips, and I almost chased it onto the sidewalk with a geyser of barf. If I told, who knew what kind of hell I'd unleash? The future played out at wild speed in my mind's eye. Pernilla slapping me, breaking off her engagement, my name turning up on Rumordale.com, the disappointment in my dad's eyes, then anguish when Pendergast leaned on the mayor to fire him from the job he'd just gotten back . . . and all because of me. *Because someone was following me on July Fourth.*

"Kevin?"

The sound of my name made me snap upright again, blood rushing to my head and making the whole world sparkle. Standing there, arm in arm, were Cheryl Blossom and Toni Topaz.

"Greetings, fellow LGBTQ warrior!" Cheryl wore a cute sundress—white with a cherry print—and oversized Chanel sunglasses. In her hand she held a crimson parasol, the ruffled canopy protecting her and her girlfriend from the sun. "What brings you out in this tragically seasonal heat?"

"I was . . . I had ice cream. With Betty. At Jordan's?" I was breathing hard, my sweat cold and everything else burning hot—and I still felt woozy.

"Are you doing okay?" Toni, her long hair a punk-rock pink, was studying me with concern. "You look kind of grayish. And greenish. And somehow also really, really flushed."

"It's probably a bacterial infection," Cheryl pronounced grimly. "The employees at that squalid little hut are a slovenly lot, and I doubt their food-storage techniques meet with FDA standards. My sweet Jay-Jay got listeria from a banana split there when we were eleven, and Mumsie forbade us from eating any confections not prepared in the kitchens at Thornhill thereafter. He had a ghastly fever, and, well." Very politely, as if it were a totally normal question, she asked, "Are you experiencing intense gastrointestinal distress?"

"On a scale from one to ten? A six." My stomach cramped again, and twisted. "Six and a half." But the pressure I felt mounting inside was more psychological than physical. I opened my mouth to excuse myself, but instead I blurted, "I think I'm going to tell Pernilla Pendergast that I made out with her fiancé."

"*What?*" Toni gasped, at the exact same moment that Cheryl exclaimed, "Oh! Good."

"*What?*" Toni repeated, doing a double take. "No, not good, Cheryl! Not good! What are you talking about?" Then she faced me, stage-whispering fiercely, "And what are *you* talking about? You know you can't do that!"

"What if I have to?" It was all I could say without revealing the reason why.

In a stout voice, Cheryl declared, "I believe that Kevin is making the right decision."

"Cheryl, babe . . ." Toni let out a groan. "I don't know what's going on with you right now, but you're not helping. For, like, a billion different reasons, he cannot do this. And honestly, I'm not even sure it's ethical."

"Of course it is." Cheryl wasn't fazed. "The deputy is a cad, a mountebank deceiving his lady love, and he deserves to be hoisted with his own petard."

"It's not *his* petard that I'm worried about!" Toni retorted through her teeth. Facing me, she held out a hand in supplication. "Kevin, think this through, okay? If you tell Pernilla what happened—if you start spreading it around *at all*—it's going to blow up into something you can't control, and it won't end well. For *anyone*. Do you get it?" Squinting at me, she continued, "Where is this coming from, anyway? We all swore—"

"I know what we swore," I snapped, more sharply than I'd intended. The night of July Fourth, a pact had been made—a pledge sworn to never speak a word about our actions ever again. "This isn't . . . it's not about that, and it's not easy for me, either." Gesturing to Cheryl, I added, "Apparently, I'm developing listeria-like symptoms from the stress! But I can't stop thinking about the fact that he's about to *get married*, and—"

"Do you really want to be responsible for outing him?" Toni cut me off, her eyes blazing. "Is that something you're prepared to do, Kevin?"

The dam burst inside me, and my vision blurred. "No. I don't . . . I don't think I am."

Because no matter who Huxley had used or was using, no matter what lies he'd told or why, *outing someone* was a line I just wasn't sure I had it in me to cross. Once I'd figured out I was gay, it didn't take very long before I felt ready—and safe enough—to tell my dad. But I still remembered that brief period like a waking nightmare. The constant pressure of lying, each simple deceit demanding another to bolster it and another to bolster *that*, the constant paranoia of being found out, of what might happen.

And I was lucky. I had a good relationship with my dad, and he'd always made it clear to me that he loved me—that every part of me mattered. But even so, it had still been scary, a confession that took months to build up to. And on the way, my doubts would flourish in every awkward silence that elapsed after my dad would ask something innocuous like "So, are there any girls catching your eye these days?"

Even if Huxley was being cruelly dishonest, even if he was being miserably unfair . . . how could I take the choice of coming out away from him, when I knew how devastating it would have been to have had that choice taken away from me?

Cheryl, of course, was far less conflicted.

"Your empathy for one of our rainbow siblings is certainly admirable, Kevin, but Hayes Huxley is philandering scum." Her tone was uncompromising. "Believe you me, if Veronica and I had not already made several large nonrefundable deposits on décor and equipment for that disastrous little fete Saturday night, I'd have insisted that we cancel." With a sniff, she added, "Let the record show that *I* am not the one who agreed to plan an engagement party without even knowing the groom's name. Alas, poor, dowdy Pernilla has betrothed herself to him, and before it's too late, she deserves to know what a tomcatting lecher he is!"

"It's not that simple," I returned curtly—and it is a testament to how upset I was that my next words were, "and you of all people should know it. Or have you forgotten what happened when you outed Moose to the whole school?"

She went stiff, and Toni clamped her lips together. Knuckles white around the handle of the parasol, Cheryl replied, "Of course I haven't forgotten. That day lives in infamy as one of my few lapses in judgment, and I not only apologized to Moose—profusely, I might add—but did as much as was within my power to make amends."

"You're right, you did. I know you did." I heaved a sigh, pressing my palms against my eyes. "I'm sorry, I . . . that was a low blow. But you saw what happened when his secret got out. His dad *terrorized* us, Cheryl! I thought one of us was going to die that night."

From that day forward, I would still occasionally wake up in a frenzied, choking horror, reliving the night that Moose and I were kidnapped from Dilton's survival bunker by a band of silent goons in rubber masks. We were forced into a clearing, where a figure dressed as the Gargoyle King demanded we play Russian roulette with two chalices of blueberry Fresh-Aid— one of which was laced with cyanide.

In the nick of time, we were saved—by Cheryl, of all people—only to then learn that the entire scenario was a fakeout. There was no poison in the cups, and the "Gargoyle King" was really Moose's father, Marcus Mason, attempting to "scare us straight."

"In keeping with a Riverdale tradition of positively Shakespearean proportions, Major Mason was a contemptible parent," Cheryl agreed, "and despite the regrets I have for forcing Moose's secret into the open, I have none over shooting his father with an arrow."

"That creep was just lucky my girl was aiming to wound instead of kill," Toni interjected darkly, giving Cheryl's arm a proud squeeze.

"But all of this is beside the point. Hayes Huxley is a

lothario, and that's not a secret that will fit into the closet," the dainty deadeye continued with an earnest expression. "You weren't at that engagement party, Kevin, but I assure you that Pernilla Pendergast is deeply in love. Her fiancé's disloyalty to her is wretched knowledge to bear." With a sigh, Cheryl allowed, "If the deputy is in a position where he does not feel safe letting his Pride flag fly, that is indeed a shameful commentary on our society. But so, too, is it a tragedy for him to mislead some poor girl into believing that she is his one and only!"

Rubbing uselessly at my temples, where a headache was starting to form, I gave a glum nod. This was more or less precisely what I'd said to Betty. "I know."

"The way you described it, it didn't take much convincing for him to haul you into that alley and stick his tongue into your mouth," Toni remarked, as lightly as one can remark such a thing. "He didn't have to do a whole lot of wrestling with his conscience, which means you're probably not the first person he's messed around with on the side."

"And if I don't tell Pernilla what Hayes is really like, he'll just keep cheating on her, making things a hundred times worse if and when the truth is finally revealed," I summarized. But I left out the other part—how if I didn't tell Pernilla, then Poison Pen *would*, and far more truths would be laid bare before the world. Ones with potentially dire consequences for all three of us, and more besides. "On the other hand, if I *do* tell her, I'll be betraying my own principles, and possibly putting another person at risk of suffering what Moose and I went through at the hands of Major Mason. Or worse."

There was a pensive silence as I looked for answers in the clouds and Cheryl gazed down at her feet. Finally, it was Toni who cleared her throat. "Not to point out the obvious, but . . . it's not 1950 anymore, guys, and not all couples are necessarily monogamous. We're just assuming all of this is information Pernilla doesn't already have, but what if she does? Maybe she knows he's also into dudes, and she doesn't care who he sees on the side. Maybe she's seeing other people, too—they might have an open relationship."

"In which case, telling her won't hurt either of them," Cheryl concluded.

"Maybe." I rubbed my mouth, the taste of strawberry syrup still clinging to the back of my tongue from the one sporkful I'd choked down earlier. "I'm not sure I can live with myself if I don't tell her . . . but if I do, and something terrible happens to Deputy Huxley as a result, all the 'maybes' in the world aren't going to help me sleep at night."

That was how I left them, standing on the sidewalk and sharing a silent conversation in worried looks, as I trudged back to my car. I sat behind the wheel for hours, waiting for a reprieve from Poison Pen that never came.

Daylight began to turn honeyed as I watched minutes slip by

on the clock, and I counted musicals all the way back to the beginning of the Tonys—and then best actresses, and then best directors—before giving up.

It was six o'clock, still two hours until my deadline, but I could think of no way out that wasn't straight through. I was going to have to swallow my principles—and hope I didn't choke on them.

The Pendergasts owned a sprawling mansion in the same part of Riverdale as Thornhill, the estate where the Blossoms had once lived, and on the way I rehearsed a dozen or more variations on how I would launch into this gut-wrenching revelation.

I would have to ring the bell and hope Pernilla answered, I decided, so I could drop the metaphorical bomb and run back to my car before she could go find a gun. I'd shout something along the lines of, *"Ask Hayes what he does in Fox Forest at night!"* I couldn't reveal who I was, and I couldn't give her any reason to focus on July Fourth in particular; if she got too curious, there was no telling what she might uncover.

If I thought I could get away with it, I'd borrow Poison Pen's own tactic and leave an anonymous note in her mailbox, but I'd been instructed to do it in person, and I wouldn't take any chances. As far as I could tell, I was the only one on the road out there in the fancy-pants hills, but for all I knew there'd been a drone chasing me in stealth mode all afternoon.

Maybe I was even being harassed by the bride-to-be herself.

Pernilla *Pen*dergast—PP—*Poison Pen*? Maybe it was *Hayes* who was being followed that night, and not me; maybe Pernilla had hired a detective to investigate the man marrying into her family fortune. Seeing us together could have made her snap, and now she wanted me to suffer.

Only, I couldn't make sense of why she'd wait this long to do something about it. And if she *did* know, she'd obviously decided to go ahead with the engagement, so why would she be so angry about those ten or fifteen minutes of (very good) kissing to go to these extremes over it? Helplessly, I relinquished the theory.

Patrick Pendergast had made several fortunes as a day trader in Manhattan before he built his third home in Riverdale's backyard, intent on using our district as a launching pad for his political ambitions. His mansion was a Georgian monstrosity of gray stone, with dozens of windows and a courtyard lined with bushes carved into razor-sharp squares. It would have made the perfect setting for a musical version of *Knives Out*, and if I'd been in a better mood, I'd have made a note about it in my phone.

As it was, I stopped my car beside a hideously tacky fountain. Staring out at the massive front door, I swallowed a dry lump in my throat.

Just as I was reaching for the door handle, my phone buzzed.

> OMG have you seen Rumordale.com yet?? TELL ME YOU'VE SEEN WHAT'S ON RUMORDALE.COM!! It's everywhere, Kevin!

ᐱᐱᐱ

RUMORDALE.COM
GET TO KNOW YOUR NEIGHBORS

If you heard an unexpected *thud-thud-thud-crash* sound earlier today, it's because Senator Patrick Pendergast just had his campaign shoved down a staircase for the second time in one week.

Faithful readers (or, really, anyone with a pulse and even basic access to the internet) will recall that the gubernatorial wannabe had his dirty laundry dumped out in front of his friends, his donors, and his wife at their daughter's engagement party this past weekend. What a way for the world to find out he's been bumping uglies with his not-so-single-either campaign manager, Caitlyn Carrington!

Well, today it is our giddy pleasure to report (in a Rumordale exclusive!) that a penchant for cheating men seems to be a hereditary trait among the Pendergast women! Yes, that's right—Riverdale's native son, Hayes Huxley, deputy with the Rockland County Sheriff's Office and husband-to-be of the young Pernilla—has been a gadabout cad about town.

An anonymous source sent us an email this afternoon, the subject line of which was short and to the rapier point: "Hayes Huxley is philandering scum, and his lady love deserves to know the truth." They had us at subj:, of course, but the attachments told the real story—a bonanza of salacious screengrabs, in which the social-climbing deputy flirts, propositions, and sends naughty photos to a pair of comely young ladies on two different social media sites.

So #SorryNotSorry to the Pendergast campaign, but a site's gotta do what a site's gotta do—and we GOTTA share the goods. (Pics or it didn't happen, after all.) The truly eXXXciting selfies have been tastefully blurred, because we're definitely not trying to get sued, but we think you'll get the gist.

Keep it classy, Riverdale!

I couldn't believe my eyes. The leaked exchanges, conducted via direct messages on Twitter and Instagram, left nothing to the imagination. One after another, Betty sent more links— the *Riverdale Register*, RIVW, even the *Times*—as the story spread, and a second wave of scandal crashed hard against Pendergast's embattled bid for governor.

Outside, the red-gold reflection of the evening sun flared in the mansion's windows. Frozen in place, I just sat and stared— gobsmacked. Poison Pen demanded that I reveal to Pernilla "what her fiancé is up to behind her back," and by now, she almost certainly already knew. But I'd never been told specifically to *out* him.

Maybe it was splitting hairs, but I could add nothing to the girl's misery besides a new perspective at this point. Could I get away with doing nothing? Could this miracle scandal actually get me off the hook?

As if on cue, my phone buzzed again.

Unknown ID:

> Looks like you were saved by the bell, Kevvie . . . and I'm not pleased. I wanted you to break this bulletin by yourself, but now that everybody already knows, all the fun has been taken out of making you walk the plank.

Lucky for you, I believe you might have squirmed just enough to satisfy me—for now. But don't get too comfortable. I'm still watching.

When I put down the phone again, I pressed my forehead to the steering wheel and wept with relief. Water burbled in the courtyard fountain, and a flock of birds streamed overhead, their cries distant and dreamlike; and for the first time all day, I could finally breathe.

The purpose of handing out an assignment is not to get back a pile of correct answers but to make the student learn something—and I must admit I'm a little annoyed with Kevin Keller for letting someone else do his homework. I should have made him go through with a confession, anyway . . . but I wasn't kidding when I said all the fun had been taken out of it.

It wasn't Deputy Huxley I was trying to punish, after all.

Certain people in this town have gotten away with too much for too long. They blunder in and out of people's lives, inviting danger, and rarely are they ever truly held accountable.

Remember the time Archie Andrews started beef with an actual battle-trained mercenary, and they tried to kill each other in the middle of Riverdale High? Or the time Betty Cooper gave a great big speech about moral values that prompted her own father to go on a killing spree? It boils down to reckless endangerment—and lessons never learned.

But, with apologies to Tom Keller, Michael Minetta, FP Jones, and Tom Keller again, there's a new sheriff in town, and I intend to make sure these would-be divas finally understand that actions have consequences.

When Veronica took out that security camera so there would be no evidence of her trashing her own car, she didn't think twice about the inconvenience to the parking garage, did she? How much the equipment would cost to replace, how many people and vehicles would be unsafe in the meantime.

When Jughead broke into that scrapyard, he didn't think about how easy he was making it for other thieves to follow. He wasn't thinking about how grand theft auto would raise insurance rates for the entire neighborhood.

Thanks to me, they both faced consequences.

Now, unfortunately, I don't have solid proof . . . but I'm about 99 percent certain that Cheryl Blossom is the one who pulled Kevin Keller's chestnuts out of the fire. Lucky for <u>him</u>, I'm on a tight schedule and don't have time to devise a new personalized torment with his name on it.

Unfortunately for <u>her</u>, I'm only halfway through my list—and when somebody begs for attention, sometimes you just have to give it to them . . .

—Poison Pen

PART FOUR
CHERYL BLOSSOM
TUESDAY

CHAPTER FOURTEEN

RedHotRiverdale:

Hey cutie! Luv your profile 😚

HuxBux:

Hey yourself, beautiful—I'm loving yours. Is that really you in those pictures?

RedHotRiverdale:

But of course! Who else would it be?

HuxBux:

Idk . . . a Vivian's Secret model?

RedHotRiverdale:

I'll take that as a compliment.

HuxBux:

You should. Are you really from Riverdale? Because I would definitely have noticed a girl as sexy as you before.

RedHotRiverdale:

I'm new to the area, actually. Just moved here this summer and don't really know anyone. So I surf the #Riverdale tag on social and see if interesting people pop up. Is that pathetic?

HuxBux:

Nah, I think it sounds kinda sweet, actually.

RedHotRiverdale:

Aw, well, I think YOU'RE kinda sweet

HuxBux:

If you want someone who can show you around, you've found your man. There aren't a lot of clubs, but there are some cool cafés and bars. And I know a great place to watch the stars at night. Secluded . . . romantic . . .

RedHotRiverdale:

Sounds like a dream. Are you asking me out?

HuxBux:

Maybe. Too forward?

RedHotRiverdale:

Not at all. I like a man with initiative.

RedHotRiverdale:

> Don't take this the wrong way, but I notice you've posted several pictures with you and some girl tagged @Perni_Pen . . . is that your girlfriend?

HuxBux:

> EX-girlfriend. Definitely no one you need to worry about, beautiful.

RedHotRiverdale:

> No worries here. Now, why don't you tell me a little more about this place where we can see the stars . . . and what else we can do there . . . 😼

∿∿

To be blunt, as is my wont: I have no regrets about creating a fake account and using it to catfish Hayes Huxley. Were he a gentleman of high caliber (or *any* caliber), he would have rebuffed my advances, and that would have been that. But he wasn't. And not only did he eagerly step into my honey trap, he stepped into TeeTee's as well—*at the exact same time.*

Our Kevin had been in such a state when he left us that I knew something had to be done. Guilt and stress were causing him to positively unravel—and I know from whence I speak, as these were the same pressures that nearly made me crack when Mumsie was gaslighting me over my allegedly-absorbed fetal triplet, Julian.

Bless his noble, misguided heart, Kevin knew Pernilla deserved a warning about her down-market Don Juan fiancé . . . but I began to see that in his emotional frenzy, he might easily reveal too much during a fraught confrontation. And if too much were to be revealed, it could endanger not only him, but me and my precious TeeTee as well. And that would simply not do.

TeeTee, of course, is a genius. It was she, after all, who suggested that Deputy Huxley would likely have a string of disloyal dalliances under his gun belt. The moment that Kevin was out of sight, my paramour and I began crafting false internet personae—selecting photos of models with rather obvious physical charms, and tailoring our profiles to reflect Huxley's aggressively basic interests.

Getting him to take the bait was a piece of disappointing cake.

When I met Hayes Huxley at his engagement party, he oozed egotism, the sort of unctuous character whose most casual touch makes you yearn for a bottle of hand sanitizer. But even *I* was shocked when he fell for the same ploy twice in one afternoon. The narcissistic pig thought so highly of himself that even with two gorgeous strangers—women utterly out of his league—making advances toward him at the same time, he never wondered if he might be getting set up.

In any event, the very instant I had receipts in hand proving what a reprobate he was, I sent them to Rumordale.com forthwith—done and dusted, no misgivings. With Kevin's conscience (and great big mouth) thus quieted, the potential danger to TeeTee and me was gone, and handed a fresh new scandal to play with, the local muckrakers were finally moving on from their coverage of the disastrous party at the Five Seasons.

Believe me when I say it took *several* pots of my signature calming tisane—a potent blend of organic lavender, chamomile, and passionflower, all grown and prepared on the grounds at Thistlehouse—to bring me back to my center after *that* fiasco.

I've endured far worse, it must be said—and, naturally, I maintained my customary grace under fire throughout. (Even as full-color photographs of the senator's aesthetically unpleasing backside were splashed across a screen the size of a bread truck.) But the truth is, I was severely rattled.

With our post-high-school futures just over the horizon, and our collaborative ventures at a crossroads, Veronica and I had agreed that cohosting the Pendergast-Huxley event was an appropriate way to bid each other adieu. All at once, we could not only cement the exclusive status of Red Raven Rum as a label for discerning tastes, but remind what passes for haute société in Riverdale that *we* were its reigning doyennes. To have our grand farewell to this accursed town end in such shocking disarray was . . . well, if I'm honest, catastrophe is the standard operating environment here, and we should have seen it coming.

But maybe one of us did.

Be it known that one Veronica Lodge began acting in an *extremely* suspicious manner earlier on the evening in question. After a few dazed apologies for the snafu—ex post facto—she all but vanished, leaving me to do the dirty work of soothing savage tempers and concocting plausible excuses. She has avoided me ever since, and while it is very possibly because she knows I intend to kill her, one cannot help but wonder if it isn't *guilt*.

Why she would do such a thing in the first place confounds me, but there is no explanation—regardless of how strange or unlikely—that can be dismissed out of hand where unsolved mysteries in the town of Riverdale are concerned.

When Tuesday afternoon rolled around, TeeTee and I were enjoying another of my tisanes (ginger, lemongrass, and orange peel) in the sitting room at Thistlehouse, and I was still considering Veronica as a suspect.

"But why would she sabotage her own event, babe?" TeeTee inquired, arching a single brow—like Diana's bow, drawn back for the hunt. "*Your* event. The two of you worked your butts off to make that thing come together."

"The question to ask isn't *why*," I pointed out shrewdly, "but *how*. *How* will tell us *who*, but *why* will only . . . clutter things up.

"Veronica's laptop was left unattended for long stretches of time, it is true, but never in a place where just anyone could get to it." I gazed off through the mullioned windows at the garden. "If we can figure out *how* someone could have managed to pull off the swap without being noticed, we won't need to know why—the circumstances should be enough to tell us who." Setting my mug down on the side table, I pointed out, "Remember how Betty and Jughead said they correctly deduced that Mumsie's proxy Jay-Jay was in fact Chic, whom they had all theretofore believed killed by the Black Hood?"

"Something about Sherlock Holmes, and ruling out the impossible?"

"'Eliminate the impossible, and whatever remains, however improbable, must be the truth,'" I quoted from Sir Arthur Conan Doyle's great detective. "Veronica had the best opportunity. It was her computer, and the slideshow was her idea in the first place. However unlikely, unless and until the *possibility* can be ruled out, we have to consider her a suspect."

"Fair enough." TeeTee was very clearly humoring me, and if I didn't adore her so, I'd have been quite cross about it.

Resting before her on the table was her orientation packet from Highsmith College, where classes would begin in a scant two weeks. I have to confess that I found her nervousness about it to be charming.

It was a rare thing indeed for my TeeTee to find herself in a situation where she was unsure of her footing—and her habitual confidence was the trait that had impressed me first and most about her. I had not a single doubt that she would meet this new challenge with her customary courage and capability, and would have Highsmith eating out of her hand within mere months. But it is impossible to see vulnerability in someone you love and not be moved, to not feel a sudden swelling of the heart and a desire to protect them.

And it was then, on that lingering, sweet note, that the doorbell rang . . . and a new catastrophe found its way to our front stoop.

The driveway of Thistlehouse is long, but the hallways are longer, and by the time I reached the porch it was empty—save for a plain white envelope lying on the mat. A perfect square, it was printed with both our names—mine and Toni's—and the flap was sealed with red wax. I cast a look around, but beyond leaves shaking in the wind, there was not a sign of movement.

"Who is it, babe?" TeeTee asked from behind me, and I spun around with the envelope in hand.

"An anonymous delivery." I traced the insignia pressed into the wax, an intricate double *P*. "Riverdale may lack culture and acceptable sushi, but it certainly has more than its share of denizens with a sense for dramatic gestures."

"Something about that envelope looks familiar . . ." My

paramour murmured the words under her breath, but I was already sliding a finger beneath the circlet of scarlet wax.

⌃⌃⌃

Dear Cheryl and Toni—

If it isn't Riverdale's oddest couple! To think that while Toni was growing up on the wrong side of the tracks, born into a gang and made to fight for every step forward, Cheryl was sulking in the lap of luxury, a silver spoon tarnishing in her sour little mouth. Imagine never having to want for anything, never doubting that you would live a life of comfort, and still turning out as jealous, miserable, and grasping as our Cheryl Blossom.

What a relief it is to finally be able to give voice to these words without fearing retribution at the hands of her pathetic pack of personal flying monkeys, the River Minions—oops! I meant Vixens. (You love to call yourself the HBIC, Cheryl, but what does it say about your leadership skills that only the most basic and mindless Bs in Riverdale are the ones willing to let you be in charge of them?)

And while we're on the subject, what are you going

to do next year when your Greek chorus of pitiful yes-women are no longer around to flatter your every vapid choice? You can't honestly be delusional enough to think you'll waltz into Highsmith College as a freshman and take charge of the social scene. Not with your family's notorious history. Not with your own checkered past of cult membership, mental instability, and gang affiliations.

And not with your extremely recent instance of reckless driving.

Yes, Cheryl, that's my way of saying that I Know What You Did This Summer. On the night of July Fourth, you committed a hit-and-run, slamming into a parked car while going well over the speed limit, and then just drove away.

Of course, you had your reasons for not stopping . . . and you'd better believe that I know what those reasons are—just like I know exactly where Toni was during your one-sided game of bumper cars, and what she was up to. (And, Antoinette, I must confess I'm dismayed by your backslide into lawbreaking. What would your family say? I'm sure you hope you'll never find out.)

Both of you ladies have been bad, but, Cheryl? You've been the worst. Think about all the things you'd do to keep this sordid affair under wraps, because the next time I get in touch, it'll be with an ultimatum. In the meantime, don't tell anyone else about this letter, or I'll know, and there will be <u>dire</u> consequences. Don't believe me? Check out the enclosed photographs . . .

Toodles!

—Poison Pen

∿∿∿

"*Cher.*" Snatching the page out of my hands, TeeTee first stared at it and then at me, eyes wide with horror. "This can't be real. There's no way—it has to be a hoax!"

"It's no hoax." My voice sounded as though it were coming from a long way off, and as I examined the glossy photos that had indeed been enclosed with that terrible note, my stomach plunged like a flier without any bases to catch her. "These are quite dreadfully real."

Numbly, I passed the pictures over, and then sank onto a Queen Anne chair beside the door. My blood had gone cold and thick, like the maple sap that fueled the Blossom empire, and for what must have been the millionth time since my Jay-Jay died, I wished that everything happening to me was a mere dream from which I could wake. Contrary to what the letter implied, the photographs did *not* depict the accident in question—but what they did show was more than enough to sink me and my future to the bottom of the Sweetwater.

Clearly shot with a high-grade digital camera, the first of the damning images showed a nondescript coupe parked in front of an alley at night, my featureless (and yet unmistakably regal) silhouette behind the wheel. The second of the images showed a figure in a black hood racing along the passage toward the car. The third and last image showed us speeding away—the coupe's license plate plainly visible in all its wildly incriminating glory.

Two days later, that same car was found abandoned on a residential street, and its plate number was used to trace it back to the scrapyard in Greendale from which it had been stolen.

CHAPTER FIFTEEN

Riverdale has known many tragedies, but there is no denying that July Fourth is a particularly star-crossed date in our hamlet's history. It marks the anniversary of my brother's most foul murder, as well as the homecoming parade for the remains of Fred Andrews after his devastating accident. Both men were, in their own ways, pillars of the community. Jason was scion to the Blossom fortune, as close a thing as we had to noble blood, and Mr. Andrews . . . he was the embodiment of every decent quality to which small-town life can lay claim.

Prior to my brother's death at the hands of our monstrous father—may he suffer in Hades from torments so horrible that even Hieronymus Bosch could not have imagined them—the Blossom family funded Riverdale's lavish annual Independence Day celebrations. In our grief, Mumsie and I buried this tradition along with Jay-Jay, unable to fathom feeling festive on or near that dreadful anniversary ever again.

But my heart grew three sizes when I saw how our town drew together to honor the life of Fred Andrews—how the pomp and circumstance of a simple parade served as a balm to souls that had known too much sadness. And so this summer, as I prepared to leave my youth behind, I informed the mayor that the fireworks display would be back and bigger than ever.

The Cheryl of three years ago—perhaps even just one year ago—would have planned to be front and center at the *grand jubilé*, claiming a place of honor at Pickens Park so all and sundry could pay proper tribute to her largesse. But the Cheryl of this year had somewhere else to be, a dark and secret covenant to honor that took precedence. As the citizens of Riverdale converged to watch flowers of sparkling light bloom against the night sky, the Cheryl of this year stood alone on a shadow-swept road at the edge of town.

With moonlight in my hair, and gloves of black leather shielding my fingerprints, I was waiting to take possession of a stolen car.

Headlights flashed into view a moment before I heard the rumble of the approaching engine—the very *loud* rumble—and by the time a dinged and dented two-door shuddered to a halt before me, I was already on the verge of apoplexy.

When Jughead Jones emerged from behind the wheel, I snapped, "Perhaps there's been a misunderstanding. I was led to believe that my services would be required as driver in an act of subterfuge— not a demolition derby."

"Good evening to you, too, Cheryl." Jughead's signature dispassion was as predictable as it was infuriating.

"Was there no older or louder vehicle you could have procured?" I asked next, dosing the words with sarcasm. "The gardener at

Thistlehouse uses a lawn mower quieter than this heavy metal concert on wheels!"

"Next time we can use your gardener's lawn mower, then," came his barbed reply. "Look, this was all they had, okay? We needed a car that no one would recognize and that couldn't be traced back to any of us, and this fits the bill—take it or leave it."

Leaving it, of course, was not an option, and he very well knew it. Under my withering glare, he added, "So it's a little noisy! If things go according to plan, no one will pay any attention to it, anyway."

This was possibly an even worse thing to say at such a moment, on such an occasion. If ever a phrase demanded bad luck from the universe, it was "If things go according to plan." But, squaring my jaw, I duly traded Jughead my car keys for those to the rolling munitions factory he had purloined from Greendale.

"Hopefully," I said, unable to resist a parting shot, "when people hear this artillery coming, they will assume it's just more exploding fireworks."

"That's the spirit, Blossom. Break a leg." Tossing a wave over his shoulder as he walked toward my car, Jughead called back, "Oh, and be careful—the gearshift has a tendency to catch between third and fourth."

It was a warning both prophetic and useless.

A little more than an hour later, I was behind the wheel of the stolen car, waiting at the curb just a half block down from the entrance to the Riverdale sheriff's station. My lips glossed, my hair styled in a perfect Veronica Lake wave (but without the sweep across one eye, *naturellement,* as it might inhibit my driving), I kept one hand on the gearshift, a comforting point of connection between the engine and me. A manual transmission demands precision, engagement, a light touch, and I had—of course—mastered the skill set long ago.

I felt electric that night, in total control, the same as before a major cheer competition. The air crackled with expectation, and I watched the station house with laser-like focus. When the time came, I would be ready to floor the pedal on a moment's notice.

It was then that the first curse wrought by Jughead's careless words (*"If things go according to plan"*) came down on our heads.

A prowl car, one of the cruisers used by deputies on patrol, rolled past on its way down the street. My pulse kicking up, sparks shooting straight to the center of my chest, I watched as its taillights flared . . . and it came to a stop directly across from the station house doors.

Panic is both pointless and unbecoming, and I refused to indulge it, but I did snatch up my burner phone to tap out a wee urgent text message.

[Blocked 1]:

> Change of plans. Company out front. Whatever you're doing, time to wrap it up!

[Blocked 2]:

> Copy. Will exit through alley—meet in back.

Clinging to my sangfroid, I circled the block and slowed again when I reached the rear of the building. Here, a tiny lot surrounded by chain link and razor wire housed vehicles emblazoned with the Rockland County Sheriff's Office seal. The next structure over was an urgent care center, but between it and the station house ran a slender alley.

Even as I pulled to the mouth of the narrow passage, I had my eye on the back lot, searching the shadows for two figures I expected to see there. Imagine my surprise, then, when I finally spotted them in the alley itself, directly beneath a security light fixed to the brick wall—and not five feet from the side exit.

There was no time even to text a warning. Almost the very moment I eased to a stop, the alley door exploded open, and a hooded figure burst from the station house. An alarmed shout echoed between the buildings, and then my passenger door was wrenched open, the masked fugitive leaping inside. *"Go, go, go!"*

Rubber squealed against pavement as I hit the gas, shoving the stick shift through first gear and into second as we peeled from the curb, jerking it into third when we picked up speed. Above us, percussive booms heralded the sudden unfurling of glittering red-gold fireworks—and behind us, the shocking report of gunfire drowned it out, bullets slamming into a NO PARKING sign just as we raced by.

My heart galloping, I forced the vehicle into fourth, coaxing the speedometer higher. More gunfire, the side mirror shattering, my passenger yelping and ducking for cover. I was suffused with danger and excitement, drunk on the adrenaline flooding my system. I had never felt so alive!

There was a turn ahead, and I knew we had to take it—to escape the deputy's line of sight and begin evasive maneuvers, but when I went to downshift, Jughead's parting curse worked its dark magic: The transmission caught between fourth and third, and the gear stick wouldn't budge. Hurtling for the intersection, I had a split second to make the call.

If I braked to a safer speed without reducing gears, the car would stall out, leaving us sitting ducks as I struggled to get the scrapyard reject started again. However, if I bore down and took the corner at forty miles per hour, we could roll or fishtail straight off the road.

In the end, I made the choice without thinking. Foot firmly on the gas, I yanked up the emergency brake, causing the wheels to lock; the car went into a skid, its back end lurching sideways in a clockwise spin . . . until the nose of the vehicle was aimed directly up the cross street. Releasing the brake, I let the tires grab the road again, and with a fierce chirp, we lunged forward once more.

Our car rocketed under trees heavy with midsummer green, navigating a gentle curve while the air filled with the mournful wail of police sirens in the near distance. My blood was hot with victory, with exultation, with the purest of endorphin highs. Everything felt more real than real, as if I'd finally woken up for the first time in my life.

And then.

"Cheryl, look out!" With a strangled gasp, my passenger thrust a

finger at something dead ahead—a shadow resolving into the form of an old woman with a dachshund on a leash. Caught in our headlights, she stood transfixed in the middle of the road, eyes bright with horror as we bore down at a terrible speed.

Again, there was only time to react. Twisting the wheel hard, I swerved around her at the last second—and the front end of the stolen vehicle smashed into a sedan parked along the curb. The collision was violent, the other car's wheel well caving in, its front bumper twisting and shearing free as the coupe plowed ahead. We were a bullet, glancing off and careening away, swerving and juddering as I wrestled for control.

The sirens screamed, and instead of hitting the brake, I shifted into fifth gear and put the pedal all the way to the floor. The last thing I saw before we bounced over a hill and vanished into the night was a single glimpse of the old woman in my rearview mirror—still frozen in the middle of the road . . . this time watching us disappear.

∧∧∧

"How is this possible?" TeeTee was staring at the incriminating photographs, her enchanting face perfectly gray with shock. "Cher . . . no one knew. No one even *could* have known. You were never supposed to leave the front of the station house, and you only moved the pickup to the back because of that patrol car."

"Don't you see?" I cast out a listless hand and let it fall. "It matters not, my love. Whatever brought this contemptible blackmailer to the sheriff's station that night, for whatever reason they were already lurking in the dark with a camera, the point is that they were there, and they managed to identify me!"

"Don't you think it matters just a little?" TeeTee dropped to her knees beside my chair, grasping my hand with her own. "I mean, it's a hell of a coincidence, right? And I can't place it yet, but I'd swear on a stack of Cheryl Blossom lip prints that there's something familiar about this letter."

"Familiar how?" I swiped a tear from the corner of my eye. "What do you mean?"

My beloved studied the letter again, and then shook her head with a frustrated grunt. "I don't know—I'm sorry. I swear it's on the tip of my brain, but it just won't come to me." Setting the page aside, she forced me to meet her limpid gaze. "We can figure this out, right? You weren't driving your own car, so whoever took these pictures—whether they were there looking for you or not—is someone who knows you."

"It's someone who *recognized* me," I corrected her, my mood growing darker by the minute. "And as false humility is worse than no humility at all, we might as well acknowledge that I am one of Riverdale's most recognizable residents. And this abusive epistle comes only days after I cohosted the most high-profile event of the summer. Given how that night ended, my face and name were all over the Sunday editions." Giving TeeTee's hands a squeeze, I rose unsteadily to my feet. "It wouldn't have taken more than a subscription to the *Register* to figure out who I was."

I began drifting down the hallway toward the Thistlehouse kitchens, my mind still lost in the shadows of July Fourth—still searching what lingered in my memory of that avenue beside the station house. Who else had been there? I certainly hadn't seen another person . . . but had there been a car? Maybe someone slouched in the back seat . . .

"Babe." TeeTee caught up with me. "Don't shut me out, okay? We need to talk about this! It says, '*The next time I get in touch, it'll be with an ultimatum.*' What kind of blackmailer sends a formal introduction and then waits before getting to the extortion? Why doesn't he issue his demands up front?"

"*Because he wants to make me suffer!*" I shouted, my voice shaking the teardrop crystals in our Baccarat chandelier. The words were instinctive, dredged from a place I'm not proud of—the part of me that remains from who I was before I met Antoinette Topaz. The girl I used to be would have done something exactly like this. "It's a classic technique, telling your victim you're going to hurt them . . . and then you don't, and they jump at every tiny sound, wondering when the blow will fall. By the time it does, *if* it does, it's a relief, because they've already endured worse, countless times over, in their imaginations."

TeeTee nodded thoughtfully, her eyes missing nothing as she took in my miserable countenance. "Cher, I know where your head is right now, but you're wrong. This isn't divine justice, okay? You're not paying for past sins, and you don't deserve this. Given everything you've been through—psychological abuse, emotional abuse, abandonment, *gaslighting*—it's a miracle you're anywhere near as well-adjusted as you are." Her smile, wry and knowing, made my own mouth twitch upward. "Someone is trying to terrorize you, *us*, and we have to stop them!"

"But how, my love? We know nothing about them—not even what they actually want. At least *that* might tell us something." I was morose, despondent, but felt a glimmer of warmth inside nonetheless from her hands in my hands. "Above all, I cannot fathom *how* Poison Pen could have learned what was afoot the night of July Fourth, nor *how* they could have known to be across from that alley at that precise time!"

"Cheryl Blossom!" TeeTee looked as if she wanted to shake me. "You survived having two murderers as parents, an attack by the Black Hood, and a brainwashing by Edgar Evernever. You've survived grief and torment and a near drowning, so don't tell me you're not up for fighting this . . . this Pretty Little Loser!" She thrust out a hand. "Let's rally the troops! We're not the only ones this puts in danger, babe! All of us will go down like tenpins if this freak starts telling what they claim they know. Call Betty or Jughead—or even Kevin! He owes us a favor after what we did for him."

"*Don't tell anyone about this letter, or I'll know,*'" I quoted somberly. "We can't take the chance that that's a bluff, dear heart. When Mumsie was the Gargoyle King, she had spies everywhere; Edgar got members of the Farm to inform on their friends and loved ones. For all we know, Poison Pen has been preparing for this moment ever since July Fourth—that's more than enough time to plant listening devices or hack our phones."

That fiery glint, the one that first made me fall in love, faded from TeeTee's eyes. "That's fair, I suppose. In this town, nothing would surprise me anymore." Linking her arm in mine, she allowed me to escort her along the corridor, into the kitchens. "If only there were some way we could seek help without making it obvious. Junior year, Sweet Pea and I came up with a way to pass messages through Dear Primrose. We need a system like that."

"Dear Primrose?" I echoed as I fetched our copper kettle from the hob, carrying it to the sink to be filled. A calming tisane of some sort was most assuredly in order, though I would likely have to devise a new—and *très puissant*—recipe to meet the challenges of our current ordeal. Perhaps I should add lemon balm.

"Yeah." TeeTee leaned against the counter beside me, watching as I turned the water on. "You know, the advice column in the *Blue & Gold*? I don't know where the name is from, but Betty told me it's been a mainstay in the paper since, like, the sixties, or something—just with different people writing it."

"Oh?" I was scarcely listening, quite caught in the grips of a bleak daydream about how vile I would look in my prison-issued orange jumpsuit. Another tear slipped down my cheek as I imagined it. "Who was the writer when you and Sweet Pea used it?"

"You'll never believe me," she said—but when she told me the name, I most definitely believed her. In fact, the kettle slipped from my hands and crashed into the basin as a sudden realization struck.

Whirling around, a low, electric hum feeding into my blood, I announced, "TeeTee? *I know who Poison Pen is.*"

CHAPTER SIXTEEN

"You think you're being puppet-mastered by *Ethel Muggs*?" My paramour chased after me as I stormed up the hallway, sparks flooding back into all my empty spaces. With just a shade of skepticism, TeeTee added, "Because she wrote an advice column?"

"Because she wrote an *anonymous* advice column," I clarified, snatching my parasol from the umbrella stand beside the door, "named after the primrose, a common garden flower and well-known *poisonous perennial*." Slipping my feet into a pair of stiletto booties (Louboutins, as Blossom flesh is admittedly weak where the color red is concerned), I arched a brow at my beloved. "PP? Poison Pen?"

"Okayyy." My girlfriend lingered in the entrance to the foyer, tugging somewhat nervously at the hem of her pleated skirt. "Listen, I'm not saying that I disagree, but . . . isn't that maybe, sort of, kind of a . . . reach?"

Hands on my hips, I arched a brow. "Are you forgetting that she locked poor, claustrophobic Josie in a closet, and abetted Sister Woodhouse in force-feeding my dear cousin Betty a handful of Fizzle Rocks? She has a criminal history!"

"And she apologized for all of that, remember? She even helped Betty rescue all those kids from the Sisters of Quiet Mercy."

"I remain as unmoved now as I was then," I declared flatly, pushing my sunglasses into place and taking a look in the mirror to be sure my hair and lipstick were on point. They were. "Her gestures at making amends were too little, too late, and those foul deeds are *still* not her only record of villainy!" Casting open the door, allowing sunlight to flood across the tile, I made my final (and most significant) point. "The last time I was the recipient of anonymous, threatening letters, *Ethel Muggs* was the one behind them!"

"You're talking about *Carrie: The Musical*," TeeTee concluded, finally putting her own boots on.

"Comme de juste." Turning back around, I fired a hard gaze at the bend in the drive, where it vanished behind the trees. By how many seconds had I just missed catching a glimpse of Ethel when I answered the door? "She wanted my role, and so she engaged in a campaign of anonymous harassment in order to have me removed from the cast, sending menacing letters composed of cut-up magazines. And her plan worked, I might add—I *did* lose that part." Just thinking of that whole affair filled me with renewed outrage. "This is her MO, TeeTee, and I don't believe for a moment that she has reformed from her nefarious past! Mark my words: Ethel is Poison Pen, and I am

going to put a stop to her fresh reign of terror *immédiatement!*"

"You know how much I love it when you use French for emphasis," my sweetheart remarked, joining me as I marched into the courtyard. "I guess we might as well go and see what she has to say for herself."

∧∧∧

I confess that I drove to Ethel's house with something of a lead foot—not only due to my ever-mounting fury, but because I believed there was still a chance I might overtake her en route. TeeTee maintained her doubts (although she was decorous enough to keep them to herself), but I was quite more than convinced. When she was exposed as my postal bully after the *Carrie* affair, Ethel admitted that she resented me, personally, because of my advantages. Because I "always get everything I want," or some such codswallop.

There would be no point in denying that I was born with a silver spoon in my mouth, per "Poison Pen's" odious little letter—but the tarnish on it was caused by lies and murder and manipulation, not my (admittedly) acid tongue. And while it's true that I have never known penury, I have most certainly lived most of my life in emotional privation. From birth, I was starved of any true affection or esteem that did not come either from my twin brother, or from my only occasionally compos mentis grandmother.

So, no. I did not "always get everything I wanted," and I frequently got things that no one on this earth would ever ask for: my brother's terrible death at the hands of our father, the revelation that our fortune was built on the spilled blood of the Uktena people, my mother's rise as one of Riverdale's most insidious supervillains. Despite my wealth and beauty and perfect pitch, my life was not entirely charmed. Even so, no matter how many times the Blossom name made headlines for all the wrong reasons, some people still saw no further than my privilege when they looked at me.

Clearly, the scorn with which the Poison Pen letter had been written came from someone who shared this same small-minded opinion, and no matter how I put the evidence together, it all added up to *Ethel*.

The tires of my vintage convertible gave a yelp of protest as I navigated a tight corner, going perhaps a bit too fast. At my side, TeeTee braced herself against the door and put a hand on my arm. "Try to stay calm, okay, babe? Remember, you can catch more flies with honey than with vinegar."

"And?" I retorted, shoving down on the gas and making the car leap forward. "Who wants to catch flies?"

The address that Ethel Muggs presently called home was two and a half stories of wood siding and gingerbread trim, with an ugly hatchback parked in the drive. I swooped in behind the vehicle and hit the brake only inches from its back bumper. TeeTee was still peeking through her fingers when I tossed open the door and leaped out.

"Cher?" TeeTee called after me, her tone bordering on alarmed. *"Cher."*

Striding right up to the hatchback, I put my hand on the hood. It was hot—hotter even than it should be from sitting out in the August sun—and the engine was slowly ticking away, a small puddle of fluid gathering under the chassis.

"If this rusting tin can has been parked here for more than five full minutes, I will eat those ill-groomed rosebushes!" I pointed at the offending plants, crowding together in an unkempt, weedy flower bed that bordered the front walk.

"Let's not draw too many conclusions, Detective Holmes." TeeTee held up her hands in a "slow down" gesture. "Just because someone was recently driving this car doesn't mean—"

"That she raced us back here after dropping a hateful and incendiary letter on our doorstep, just like the Unabomber?"

My love twisted her mouth to the side for a moment. "I wasn't going to invoke that extreme of an example, but sure. You know, it's possible she was—"

"Just look at this place!" I cast my eyes from the shabby garden to the overgrown yard to the grungy windows, where spiderwebs as thick as cotton batting stretched across the upper corners. "Are you telling me this isn't the abode of a murder-by-mail psychopath? If we were to open that garage door right now, there'd be no telling what horrors might come spilling out!"

It was precisely then, of course, *of course*, that the garage door ratcheted up with a great *whoosh*, revealing Ethel Muggs herself. She was clutching a cardboard box to her chest, her face was pink and sweaty, and her eyes were practically aglow with a combination of surprise and naked rage at the sight of me in her driveway. "Cheryl? What the hell are you doing here?"

"I might ask you the same thing!" I shot back in a frigid snarl.

Ethel blinked. "I live here. This is my house?"

"Right." I lifted my chin. Another valuable lesson from my worthless father: *Never back down.* "Where have you been today, Ethel? If you don't mind my asking—which you only would if you had something to hide."

Ethel glanced from me to my paramour, and then back again, wrapping her arm just a little tighter around that cardboard box. "I've been here. Mostly."

"This rolling carnival attraction of an auto tells a different story." Indicating her car, I took a threatening step closer, and Ethel drew back, reaching for the pull cord that would slam the rolling garage door down between us.

TeeTee intervened at the last second.

Dragging me backward, she gave Ethel a wide, disarming smile—although I could tell that the muscles in her cheeks were a trifle strained. "Sorry to bother you, Ethel, but we were hoping you could help us with something."

"Help you with what?" The girl was on high alert, her eyes

darting from one of us to the other. Our window of opportunity was closing. "What do you want?"

"The jig is up, Lady Zodiac!" I spat fiercely. "We know you're the one who wrote that horrid little letter, so you might as well—"

"*Babe.*" TeeTee—my love, my only—gave me a wide-eyed look, and through her teeth she advised, "Let's dial it back a little here. Less vinegar, more honey?"

"What are you talking about?" Ethel demanded, her fingers still wrapped around the rolling door's pull cord. "What letter?"

That friendly smile back in place, her tone measured, TeeTee said, "We got a letter today. It wasn't signed, but it was . . . it said some pretty unfriendly things."

Ethel's expression hardened, but her grip on the cord went slack. "And you thought maybe I sent it."

I was about to snap out a reply, but TeeTee anticipated my reaction, and shushed me with a finger before I could speak. "It wouldn't be the first time you wrote something meant to intimidate Cheryl, without putting your name to it."

"This is about what happened during *Carrie*?" Ethel let go of the pull cord, but if anything, her expression only became harder. Wrapping both arms around that curious box, she huffed, "That was two years ago, Cheryl—more than two years! We've actually graduated, and you're still holding on to that? Grow up."

The disgust in her voice was palpable, and it awoke something inside me that I didn't like: insecurity. When I'd first read Poison Pen's words, I was too racked by the squalling winds of distress to feel much else, and then, as I pieced together the clues that identified my perfidious tormentor, anger had taken over. But now, caught suddenly in the net of Ethel's distaste, some of the letter's other harsh rebukes began to sting as well.

"Jealous, miserable, and grasping . . . only the most basic and mindless Bs in Riverdale are the ones willing to let you be in charge of them . . . You can't honestly be delusional enough to think you'll waltz into Highsmith College as a freshman and take charge of the social scene." It was uninventive, schoolyard spite, and yet every word of it cut me to the core. Because, deep down, I knew every line was true.

I'd ruled the Vixens, and the rest of Riverdale High, with fear and intimidation—because I'd never learned how to gain loyalty out of simple respect. Because I'd spent my whole life being told I was worthless, unlikable, *unlovable*. And I truly had no idea what I would do when the social slate was wiped clean and I had to start over.

It felt as though we had received our diplomas just yesterday, and already Ethel had recovered from any sense of awe she felt in my presence. She'd shrugged off the influence I'd spent close to two decades cultivating in Riverdale, and instead of deference, she was treating me with a withering contempt. To my embarrassment, I recoiled from it, because in some dark, treacherous part of my heart, I believed—I *knew*—that I deserved it.

Shame burning my face, I still summoned up my blood. *Never back down.* "What's in that box?"

"What box?" Her eyes went a little blank. Then, with a glance at the object she held in a veritable stranglehold against her breast, she said, "Oh, you mean *this* box? Nothing. It's nothing, just . . . books."

Even TeeTee's eyes narrowed at this. "You want to try that again, Ethel?"

"I don't owe you an explanation—either of you!" the girl barked, face going from pink to red. "You come over here, making snide comments about my mom's car and how our house looks, and now you're treating me like some kind of . . . suspect? Why don't both of you go jump in a vat of blueberry Fresh-Aid?"

Ethel stepped forward, slamming the garage door down behind her, shoving past us and stomping for the hatchback. Hot on her heels, TeeTee tried for a friendlier tone. "You're right—I'm sorry. I didn't mean to be rude, it's just . . . the letter we got was pretty upsetting, and we've been on edge ever since. We just really want to know who's behind it."

"That's not my problem," Ethel shot back, unlocking the car.

"No, it's not." TeeTee sounded agreeable, but her eyes were

cool and careful. "Still, I mean, come on, Ethel. You *did* send those anonymous notes to Cher and Kevin—and you did kind of kidnap Jughead and force him to kiss you that one time. You can't act like we're totally off base for thinking you might do something shady again."

"Oh, are we holding other people's pasts against them?" The girl spun around with a venomous look. "Because if we're getting into it, your lists are longer than mine."

"Also fair," TeeTee allowed, and then she and I exchanged a glance—because there were certain things in our past of which Ethel, even if she were Poison Pen, did not and could never know. Such as what really happened to my uncle Bedford last Thanksgiving. "We're not trying to sling accusations."

"Speak for yourself." Crossing my arms over my chest, I glared down at Ethel. "If you ask me, we've found our Gossip Ghoul—and, I notice, nothing she's said actually amounts to a denial, either."

Ethel let out a furious snort. "You are unbelievable, Cheryl, you know that?"

"Also not a denial." Primly—and politely, it must be acknowledged—I said, "You wouldn't mind if I took a teensy peek at what's inside that mysterious little box you're toting, would you?"

"It's not *mysterious*." Ethel scowled so profoundly I feared her whole face might cramp. Had she not been acting like a spy caught smuggling contraband out of East Berlin, I'd probably not even have noticed what she was carrying at all, but now it was all I could think about. "I already told you, it's just books."

"Good, then you don't object!" A lifetime of cheer, gymnastics, and archery results in upper arm strength that is nothing to joke about, and Ethel Muggs didn't stand a chance when I grabbed the box and wrenched it from her grasp.

I'm not sure what I expected to find when I opened the cardboard flaps, exposing its contents to the light of day. Square envelopes? Crimson sealing wax? But Ethel clearly wanted to keep it a secret and—given the circumstances—that was the only impetus I needed to take a look. By force. Plunging my hand inside, I grabbed the first item that met my fingers and pulled out—

"A book?" I stared at it, like some enchanted totem that might magically revert to its real form in my grasp. On the cover, a couple clung to each other in a sensuous embrace, their moist, pouting lips only inches apart.

"I *told* you," Ethel snapped furiously, snatching it away from me.

I pulled out another. Its cover centered a man's bare and well-muscled torso, unbuttoned jeans slung low on his hips. "*The Duke's Wager*? What sort of duke wears—"

"*Give me that!*" Ethel shouted, yanking the second book from my hand as well, throwing it back into the box and then tossing all of it into the back seat of her car. Whirling on us, flames crackling in her eyes, she snarled, "Are you *satisfied*?

Did you get what you came for? You can go back to your friends now and laugh all about how you caught me with a bunch of dirty novels. Congratulations!"

Flustered, I blinked rapidly behind my designer lenses, feeling compelled to say something. "Ethel . . . there's no shame in reading those books, not if it's what you enjoy. My nana Rose has a whole library—"

"Oh, wow, thanks for your approval," Ethel cut me off. "So good to know this won't end up being one more of the completely arbitrary reasons you've ostracized me my entire life." Slamming the car door, she added, "And just for your information, these aren't even mine. I'm bringing them to my mother so that she has something to read. *In the hospital.*"

"Your mother's in the hospital?" Somehow, this was the only response I could manage.

"*Yes,* Cheryl! She is! Are you seriously kidding me right now?" She stared as if this were something I ought to already know—as if we'd finally come upon some random thing that she *did* believe was "my business." Thrusting a hand out at her dilapidated home, Ethel exclaimed, "My mom was in a really bad accident last month! Some junkies broke into our house, and she snapped her leg in three places falling down the stairs while trying to escape. It was in the *Register* and everything!"

Shaking my head a little, I managed a shrug. "Well, I'm obviously sorry for your misfortune, but print media is dying, and this is the first I'm hearing about it."

"I created a PleaseFundMe to help cover her medical bills and sent the link to the *entire Riverdale High listserv*. Including you!" Ethel glowered at me. "Toni even donated to it, by the way."

When I glanced over at TeeTee, I could see that this was true. My paramour gave a nod of confirmation, saying, "It was a few weeks ago. I thought we'd talked about it, but . . . maybe we didn't?"

Turning back around, I once more took in those sad rosebushes, the spiderwebs, and the grasses gone wild in the front yard. "Is that why your property is in such lamentable condition? There's no one to take care of it?"

"Are you for real?" Ethel ranted. "Do you . . . do you even hear yourself when you speak?" Shouldering me aside, hard, she wrenched open the door of the hatchback again and flung herself behind the wheel. "I have to get to the hospital. My mom's physical therapy appointments take forever, and they're horrible, and having me there is important to her." Then she sat for a moment, glaring at me with expectation. When I said nothing, she shouted, *"Would you mind moving your car?"*

Her tone was so hostile, I jumped an inch in my Louboutins, and then hurried automatically for the convertible. Backing hastily out of the drive and into the street, TeeTee and I idled at the curb while Ethel sped away up the block. It was only as she vanished from sight that I finally realized she never *had* denied being Poison Pen.

CHAPTER SEVENTEEN

"Cher? Babe? Everything all right in there?"

I was so deep in the spiral of my thoughts that TeeTee's voice sounded as though it were coming from far off. Removing my sunglasses, I took an honest look at my own face in the rearview mirror, and for the first time in a while I wasn't sure I liked what I saw. "Am I a bad person?"

TeeTee straightened up, giving me a reproving frown. "Cher—"

"No, please. Just . . . listen." Folding my hands in my lap, I said, "We both know I have a history of being somewhat ruthless. And selfish." To silence her perfunctory protest, I hastened to add, "No, it's true. I'd like to think I've changed—I believe I have—but . . . is it ever possible to truly make up for your past?"

"Cheryl Blossom, you listen to me." TeeTee faced me across the gearshift. "Your whole life, you've let your parents control your self-image. Even when you thought you were creating your own person, you were just trying to become someone who defied the limitations they said you had." She reached out and put a hand on my cheek, her caress gentle and full of love. "But since we've known each other, I've seen you *truly* change. You're not the girl I met two and a half years ago—you're not even the girl I moved in with—but you're still the girl I love. And every day I see how much you care and how much you want to keep being a better person."

"Ethel still hates me," I pointed out dully. "Poison Pen still hates me."

"The thing about growing as a person is that it changes who you are, but not who you were. And so, yeah, the past is set and you can't undo it, and there are people who won't be willing to give you a second chance, and that's their right—but your past isn't your future, babe." She smiled, and it was the sun breaking through the clouds, a familiar melody played in the dark. "Your future is a blank page, and every day is a new chance to write a better story."

And it was, of course, on this hopeful note that my phone sounded with an incoming message, and shattered our little moment of peace—for good.

Unknown ID:

That was an embarrassing display, CherCher. Rolling up on Ethel Muggs and bullying her over a hunch? And all you managed to prove is that you're even more self-centered than I thought. Don't you ever get tired of your own reckless arrogance? Everyone else does. In fact, as far as I can tell, there's only one person in Riverdale who actually likes you . . . and you're determined to sink her to your own level.

Unknown ID:

Well, if you really want to drag Toni down with you, here's your chance—because of course you're not the only one I've got dead to rights. On July Fourth, you might have been the driver of a stolen car . . . but your girlfriend was one of the thieves who stole it. And, naturally, I have the proof . . .

Unknown ID:

[ToniTopaz1.jpg] [ToniTopaz2.jpg] [ToniTopaz3.jpg]

The pictures that popped up on my phone made my blood run colder than Sweetwater River the winter I almost drowned. Grainy but distinct, likely taken by a security camera, they showed my beloved TeeTee—along with Riverdale's very own boho hobo, Jughead Jones—sitting in her car at a specific intersection in Greendale. Time-stamped the night of July Fourth, even if they didn't prove beyond a shadow of a doubt that they were responsible for the scrapyard break-in, the photos were damning enough.

They put her at the scene, whence a car—later recovered in Riverdale, and of which there were additional photographs showing yours truly behind the wheel—was hot-wired and driven off the lot. Even without a summary explanation from Poison Pen, these pictures were suggestive enough that Sheriff Keller would have to bring us all in for questioning, should he get hold of them.

And given what that stolen vehicle was connected to—the hooded figure bursting out of the station house in full view of Deputy Huxley, the chaotic getaway ride, the hit-and-run with the parked car—there was no telling how serious the consequences might be.

Unknown ID:

I promised you an ultimatum, Cheryl, and here it is. I'm going to send you one more file, a video, and you have a choice: Either you upload it to ViewTube and share it on ALL your social media accounts . . . or I tell everyone what you and Toni did on July Fourth.

Unknown ID:

You've got money and lawyers, and maybe you can weather the storm . . . but can your girlfriend? She's been in gangs, she's got unsavory connections, and, why, I believe she even has a rap sheet! She's old enough to be tried as an adult, too. Sure hope her family doesn't need her around for the next ten to twenty. I'll give you two hours to decide, and then I'm deciding for you. Toodles!

When the video loaded, just the freeze frame made my hands shake and my eyes blur with tears—because I knew exactly what it was. Beside me, TeeTee gasped, squeezing my hand in hers like she wanted us to fuse together. "*No.* How . . . how could they have gotten hold of this? I thought if these recordings still existed, they'd be in the hands of the FBI!"

"Obviously not." I wasn't trying to be argumentative. Once again, my heart had dropped out of my chest, and I was numb all over. Numb, but still crying. What a strange sensation. "It's a masterstroke—checkmate in three moves. If I don't post this, both of our futures are forfeit."

"You can't."

"But if I do," I observed, almost mechanically, "I'll be humiliated. The video will follow me the rest of my days, coming up any time someone does an internet search for my name forevermore. It won't destroy me . . . but it *will* haunt me."

"You *can't do it*, Cher!" TeeTee grabbed me by the shoulders. "This is . . . it's extortion! There has to be some way we can still figure out who sent this. Those pictures of me in Greendale had to have been taken by a security camera at the service station across the street—it's the only explanation."

"So what, who cares?" Listless and lethargic, I was sinking

into the quicksand of depression. "Even if they were taken by the Hubble Telescope, it doesn't change a thing."

"Listen to me!" TeeTee's voice took on a sharp edge I'd rarely heard from her. "Whoever's doing this . . . somehow, they were behind the station house at the exact right time. Someone was back there with a camera for some reason, and we just have to figure out why!"

"Why doesn't matter." I almost smiled, repeating my own words from earlier in the day—before our lives had been blown to bits. "All that matters is how. As in 'how I'm going to manage this.'"

"No, as in *how* did this freak put all of this together? How did they get that service station to hand over their security footage? If we can talk to the owners, maybe—"

"Don't you see, my love?" I faced her at last, my eyes swimming. "There are limitless possibilities. The photographer who caught me red-handed could have been an opportunist—or someone who was following me with such stealth that I never saw them. They could have bribed the service station, or hacked their data storage. It could be someone so rich and powerful that they have a finger in every pie from here to Seaside, or a dozen people working together like some dreadful plot by Agatha Christie." Tears streamed down my cheeks, splattering on our joined hands. "It doesn't matter. None of it matters. In two hours either I walk through the fire, or we both burn."

"I won't let you sacrifice yourself for me." My TeeTee, my love, my only, swallowed hard as her voice caught. Tears glimmered in her wide brown eyes and she said thickly, "When I agreed to be part of what went down on July Fourth, I knew the risks—we all did—and one of them was that we might get caught." With a rough laugh, she bit her lip. "Hell, I did so many things with the Serpents that could have landed me in either juvie or jail . . . it's almost amazing it took this long. I've always been prepared to face this kind of music, babe, but you're not. Highsmith was a great dream while it lasted, but I won't let you carry this video around on your back for the next fifty years just to be noble."

My paramour's words struck a chord, at last, and I straightened my spine. I was a Blossom—not like my nefarious father, or my amoral mother, but like my nana Rose: a survivor, capable of making it through worse than the worst. "No one 'lets' me do anything," I declared, putting some fire into my tone at last. "Until I say otherwise, I'm still the HBIC in this flaming dumpster of a town, and I make my own decisions. Of the two of us, *you* are the one who is making the noble choice, TeeTee. Through blood, sweat, tears, and all-nighters, you earned your rightful place at Highsmith. My acceptance was a foregone conclusion, a legacy built on generations of filthy lucre."

"Babe." TeeTee was crying, and she was beautiful. "You can't do it."

"It's already done." I made the last keystrokes on my phone and set it down, trying to smile, although my insides were wobbling and ready to burst. "If I could only save myself or only save you, I would choose you every time. I do choose you. Always."

Leaning closer, pressing my forehead to hers, we cried. Together. And I knew that if I could earn the love of someone like Antoinette Topaz, despite my past, I could live this down someday, too.

Here's my favorite thing about an ultimatum: It's a Choose Your Own Adventure for the soul. I designed the frying pan, and I started the fire, but Cheryl had to choose which one would cook her goose—and the meal of her misery is truly delicious.

You might wonder why I would go to all that trouble when I could simply have twisted her arm instead—the way I did for Veronica, Jughead, and Kevin. Well . . . while you've no doubt heard the saying "Let the punishment fit the crime," I believe in a justice that's a little more poetic: Let the punishment fit the criminal.

Anyone who knows our Miss Lodge knows that her reputation as a suave, stylish businesswoman is what she values most. Well, thanks to me, everyone in the state now knows her as the Hostess with the Mostest Faux Pas. Imagine humiliating the father of the bride-to-be and having no excuse to offer. There goes her personal brand! I hope Barnard likes charity cases.

Jughead Jones fancies himself Riverdale's only true counterculturist. And yet he's depended for years on the protection and social cache that comes from being besties with this pathetic town's number one son, Archie Andrews. So what sentence could be more suitable than forcing him to sever that umbilical cord himself? I mean, it's time he walked the walk.

Despite his lectures about respecting the privacy of others, Kevin Keller showed a remarkable lack of respect for Pernilla Pendergast's relationship. And we all know he was spending "quality personal time" with Moose on the down-low, even when Moose and Midge were together. We in the biz call that a "pattern of behavior." So, Kevin's punishment was to do unto others exactly as he's always said never to do unto others.

And that brings us back to Cheryl. Little Miss Prim-and-Proper. Little Miss HBIC. Despite a thriving relationship, a fabulous home, and more money than she could spend in a lifetime, the only thing Cheryl really values is public perception. So when I got my hands on a video of her exposing her most secret vulnerability, you'd better believe I made her publicize it.

As for Toni Topaz . . . okay, I went a little easy on her. I made her Cheryl's bait—which was somewhat sadistic, yes, but far less of a punishment than what she maybe deserved. I have my reasons, though, and when I'm ready to explain, you'll see why.

In the meantime, it's four down and two to go— and we're finally reaching the dark, ugly heart of this whole affair. For all her posturing and bravado, Cheryl Blossom is still more honest than Riverdale High's golden boy, Archie Andrews. He's the reason all this is happening, after all.

And it's high time he finally answered for his sins.

—Poison Pen

PART FIVE
ARCHIE ANDREWS
WEDNESDAY

CHAPTER EIGHTEEN

RUMORDALE.COM
GET TO KNOW YOUR NEIGHBORS

BREAKING: They say that when it rains it pours, and this week? The gossip is coming down like a biblical flood. Remember, kiddies, your seat bottom cushion doubles as a flotation device—and you're going to need it!

In just the past few days, we've covered fabulous parties, political scandals, and dynastic infidelities of the upper crust. (Like father, like son-in-law . . . at least where the Pendergasts are concerned!) Well, earlier today, Cheryl Blossom—pampered local princess and heiress to the Blossom Maple Syrup fortune—decided to reclaim her share of the unflattering limelight by posting a deeply weird and EXTREMELY cringe-worthy video on social media.

Now, we here at Rumordale have seen all the conspiracy theories (and, holy moly, you people are creative), but so far there is no confirmed explanation for the gaffe. Miss Blossom herself has refused to respond to requests for information, but the strange video has been up for several hours as of this writing, and she has yet to take it down.

We've embedded the file below, but for those who appreciate or require a transcript, one has also been included. Happy viewing, Rumordalers.

∧∧∧

I can't say that I've ever truly understood what makes Cheryl Blossom tick. In my experience, it was always easier—and smarter—to just get out of her way, rather than try to figure her out. The only predictable thing about her was that whatever she did, she'd do it louder than anybody else.

Still, I was pretty shocked when that super-personal video popped up on Rumordale.com, and it turned out to be sourced from one of Cheryl's own accounts. Halfway through my first viewing, I knew I should turn it off . . . but somehow I couldn't. It was like watching a car accident in slow motion.

It showed Cheryl, seated on a folding chair in some dark little room, a bright light shining in her face. She wore this big, creepy smile, her eyes watery and a little glazed, and there was someone sitting across from her—in the shadows, his back to the camera. All I could make out was that he had red hair, like mine. Like Cheryl's. But what really tripped me up was how the video started.

Swiping a tear from the corner of her eye, Cheryl said, "Jay-Jay, you know how much I cherish this time that we have together. Not so very long ago, I believed I would never see you again, and this—getting to be with you—is a miracle. It's my very dreams come true."

The first time I watched it, I did a double take—because Jason Blossom, or "Jay-Jay," as Cheryl always called him—was *dead and gone.* Not missing, but, like . . . *very, very dead and gone.* Dead and gone, as in, we'd all sent his roaring funeral pyre adrift down Sweetwater River in a genuine Viking send-off late last fall. And Cheryl had lit the match herself.

The first thing I did was check the date in the corner of the video, thinking it must have been recorded before all that business went down. And I did a triple take, because the stamp said it had been recorded near the end of our junior year—during the height of Edgar Evernever's stranglehold on Riverdale's lost souls.

On my computer screen, Cheryl continued, "I will forever be in Edgar's debt for making our moments together possible, dear brother, and he says that I need to be honest with you. Completely honest, or my spirit will always be heavy with deceit, and I will never be able to achieve true peace."

And *that's* when I finally figured out what I was watching. Betty had told me about Evernever's spellbinding tricks, how he would convince his followers they were seeing things they couldn't—like loved ones they'd lost. Under the power of hypnotic suggestion, he'd even made Betty believe she was talking to her own shadow self . . . until she'd figured out it was really her sister, Polly.

At some point, he'd gotten Cheryl to believe she could converse with her dead brother—and not in some metaphorical sense, either, but *actually conversing* with the *actual corpse* of her *actual brother*—and through hidden cameras he had recorded everything she'd said.

"I love you, Jay-Jay, you know that," Cheryl proclaimed, peering with tear-filled eyes at what remained of Jason Blossom—and I shuddered involuntarily, grateful the stuffed cadaver was hidden by shadows. "But . . . I also hate you." Her voice caught and broke. "Our whole lives, you've been the Blossom everyone loved. The good son, the good friend . . . the good twin. You have no idea how hard it's been, always falling short, only ever hearing Mumsie and Daddy acknowledge my existence when they needed me to know what a disappointment I was, how I didn't measure up to your example. They preferred you—everyone has *always* preferred you. I've never been good enough. Because of you, they never loved me."

Her shoulders bent inward, and she began to sob. "After they found that body in the river, the one everyone thought was you,

Mumsie said she'd lost the wrong child—that *I* should have died instead. And what I finally realized is . . . is that she's *right*."

And that's where the recording ended.

Maybe I didn't know her as well as I thought I did, but I couldn't understand why the Cheryl Blossom I'd gone to school with for my whole entire life—a girl who wanted everyone to think she was bulletproof—would broadcast something like this. Jason's death had hit her really hard, we all knew that. But even when her grief had been fresh, she'd tried to keep anyone from catching her in a moment of weakness.

She hadn't always been the nicest person in town, and there were plenty of former Riverdale students who were flocking to the video like hyenas to a fresh kill. The message boards on Rumordale.com were filled with gleefully cruel comments from folks who'd felt bullied by Cheryl—gloating about her painful, private confession. Unable to stomach any of it, I finally shut my laptop.

For a minute, I considered texting Cheryl, just to see if she was okay—but that was the only kind of attention she hated, and I wasn't in the mood to deal with verbal abuse for trying to be nice. In fact, after getting dumped by my best and oldest friend only a couple of days earlier, I wasn't in the mood to do much of anything but feel sorry myself. And my task for the day made *that* a whole lot easier.

I was in my office at the back of the community center, where I was supposed to be packing my things up. After a year of grueling work at the former El Royale, investing everything I had into it and more, the time had finally come for me to say good-bye. And not on the terms I'd planned, either. What I'd wanted was to create a place in Riverdale where kids could grow and learn, to develop pride in themselves and their town—a place they could leave in better shape than when they came in.

The irony of it all was almost more than I could take.

In a way, after everything that had happened, the truth was that a part of me was ready to let go. I'd given the Fred Andrews Community Center everything I could, but it still hadn't been enough. And with Munroe's departure for Notre Dame just around the corner, the place would never be the same again.

It was while I was trying—and failing—not to get choked up taking photos down off the wall that there came a knock at my door. "Hope I'm not interrupting. I can practically hear those two thoughts rattling around in that great big head of yours."

When I looked up, Munroe Moore was leaning against the doorframe, already dressed head to toe in official Fighting Irish gear. For the first time all day—all week, really—I felt something like happiness, and I couldn't help but smile. "Hey, man!" I pushed back from my desk and went to greet my soon-to-be-former partner. "What are you doing here? We already threw you a going-away party—didn't you get the hint?"

"Years of boxing gave me a pretty thick skull, Andrews."

Playfully, he rapped his head with a boulder-sized fist. "I don't really do hints anymore."

"Well, you're not getting a second party. The center can't afford it."

"Don't take this the wrong way, but I hope that's a promise." He flashed a broad grin. "I still haven't gotten the taste of burned cake and canned fruit punch out of my mouth from the last one."

"Hey, listen, I baked that cake myself!"

"I know. And I still haven't forgiven you for it." Glancing around the office, he shook his head. "Believe it or not, I'll miss this place."

"I know what you mean," I told him. "We built the center together, man—from the ground up. You ever wonder what Sketch Alley would've been like without us?"

"I guess we'll see. I'll be back for Thanksgiving . . . maybe I'll swing by the place." With a wry smirk, he asked, "Think there'll be another shoot-out this year? Like old times?"

"Let's hope not." I laughed, because he meant it as a joke . . . but in the back of my mind, all I could hear was Jughead shouting accusations.

"You opened the community center to help disadvantaged kids, and then you almost got them all killed on Thanksgiving!" At the time, I'd been so surprised—and hurt—by the things he was saying that I hadn't been able to respond. It's not like Jug and I had never fought before, and they weren't even the worst things

he'd ever said to me . . . but they'd landed like a blow to the gut.

It was only later, his words spreading under my skin like a bruise, that I started to realize how ashamed I was. Because he'd been right.

I did get FP shot. And I was the reason all those kids were in danger on Thanksgiving—even if it had happened, in a sickly ironic way, because I'd been trying to keep them *out* of danger. But then, that had been Jug's point: that I get other people in trouble because I don't consider the consequences of my actions until it's too late. And given the cloud I was leaving the center under, how could I even think of defending myself?

Looking before I leap: a pretty basic life skill I was going to need to develop, now that I'd run out of people to count on when the chips are down. What's embarrassing is that I'd only just started to realize how much I've always thought of myself as the bottom line—life's goalie, or something like that—the last line of defense. The only guy still standing when everybody else is down for the count.

I definitely believed that about myself when I formed the Red Circle, and when I took on Dodger Dickenson, patrolling the streets like a vigilante. Well, not *like* a vigilante; I *was* a vigilante. I believed that if I didn't take charge of the fight, there would be no fight at all. *"You've got a hero complex, Archie."*

Now my dad was gone, and Munroe was leaving—as well as Ronnie and Betty—and Jughead wasn't returning my calls or texts. Even when I told him he'd had a point. So it looked like finally, just as I was considering my own changing future—just as I was starting to truly appreciate how much I'd counted on my friends—I was completely on my own. For real.

"But, listen," Munroe was saying, and I tried to shake off all those heavy shadows and pay attention. "The real reason I stopped by is just to say thanks—again. For being there for Malcolm when I couldn't be. This was a hard year for him."

For just an instant, I went stiff, my heart skipping the same beat it always did whenever someone brought that subject up. Munroe didn't know everything I'd done to protect Malcolm while he was at his orientation in Indiana this summer. And he never could.

Eyes down on my desk, I shrugged. "I already told you, no thanks are necessary. The kind of trouble he could've been in . . . all I did was the right thing."

"Maybe. But maybe you'd be surprised how many people won't do the right thing, even when it's easy." Munroe was serious, his voice deep and quiet. "Anyway, it meant a lot to me. This scholarship to Notre Dame, this opportunity . . . it's something I thought I'd only ever be able to dream about. And when it became real, I had to face the fact that it meant leaving my brother and my grandma—and that almost made me give it up."

"I'm glad you didn't," I said.

"Me too." He grinned again. "My grandma would've kicked

my butt all the way to Indiana herself if I'd tried." His expression becoming sober again, he added, "But they're everything I've got left in the world, and the fact that they had you in their corner when they needed someone . . . it means a lot to me, Archie—more than I can say."

"It's cool, Munroe." The conversation was making me squirm, my leg getting jumpy under the desk, and I did my best to bring it to an end. "As far as I'm concerned, Malcolm is part of my family. And you know how I feel about family."

"I do. But you looking out for him isn't a favor I'll forget." He made me sit with this for a long moment before he straightened up, giving the doorframe a thwack with the side of his fist. "I should go. My grandma's fixing an epic meal tonight— part of her *very* extended good-bye." He turned to leave, but then turned back just as fast. "Oh yeah, I almost forgot—I grabbed the mail on my way in. Old habits die hard."

Handing the stack over, he gave me a salute, and then walked out, whistling the Notre Dame Victory March. Chuckling in spite of myself, I turned to the usual mess of cards and letters the center received every day. There were two pro-Pendergast leaflets and one anti-, three offers of "no risk" credit lines, and an ad for a carpet retailer addressed to the El Royale's previous owner.

Then, at the bottom of the stack, I found a plain square envelope with my name on it. There was no return address, and the flap was sealed with wax. Immediately, my mind flashed on the stories we'd all heard about Ascension Night—when our parents received ornate invitations to a deadly round of Gryphons and Gargoyles at Riverdale High back in the nineties.

As far as I knew, Penelope Blossom was no longer a threat . . . and yet I had my jaw set tight as I pressed my thumb against the wax disc and popped it loose.

$$\wedge\wedge\wedge$$

Dear Archie,

Do two wrongs ever make a right? More importantly: Do you think you're even capable of stopping at just two wrongs? History would say no . . . but then, your grades make it pretty clear that you are no student of history.

There isn't much I can tell you about yourself that Jughead didn't already say last Sunday. (Oh, yes, I was there—and I was having the time of my life. You should have seen the look on your face!) I certainly hope you were listening to that particularly educational lecture, because it's time to put some of those lessons to the test.

And, trust me, AA, this is one test you really don't want to fail.

One fateful evening earlier this summer, you stole official police evidence right out from under Sheriff Keller's nose. Oh, you did it for all the right reasons, of course . . . But in typical Archie fashion, the only thing on your mind was All the Right Reasons. You didn't think twice about what would happen when—<u>not if</u>—you got caught.

For a boy who barely survived juvie, you sure seem determined to get locked back up again. Lucky for you, things worked out in your favor this time. Also lucky for you, I don't plan on ratting you out to the sheriff. Yet.

We're going to play a game, Archie Andrews. If you win, I'll keep your secret, but if you lose? Well, I'm sinking your battleship—and I'll make sure that it goes down with all hands on deck. That means you, Jughead, Veronica, Kevin, Cheryl, Toni, and even your bestest girl, Betty. Maybe especially Betty.

See, I know everything, right down to the nitty-gritty details—what you did, and what your friends did as a result. So unless you want to be responsible for ruining all those lives, you'll do what I say. Stay alert, Coppertop, because you'll be hearing from me again soon with the rules. And in the meantime, you'd better keep your mouth shut. I've got you in my sights, and if you tell anyone about this letter, I'll know . . . and I'll make you regret it.

I'm watching you.

—Poison Pen

CHAPTER NINETEEN

The page came loose from my hand and dropped to the floor, and my throat closed tight. Mechanically, I turned to a framed picture on my desk—me and Betty, grinning into the camera, holding popsicles crossed like swords. It had been taken on June 23—right before all this was set in motion.

"Say 'all for one and one for all!'" Kevin instructed, holding up the camera.

"Can we say that after you take the picture?" Betty gestured with her popsicle. "Otherwise our mouths will look all weird."

"Too late, your mouths already look weird." Kevin turned the digital display to face us. "I took, like, ten shots while you were talking just now."

Betty narrowed her eyes. "Just take one where we say 'cheese' like normal people, or you're going to be eating that camera."

"Okay, you're starting to sound a little bit hostile, and that's not exactly a festive—" Kevin cut himself off when he saw the look on Betty's face. "Uh, yeah . . . say 'cheese!'"

"Cheese!" Betty and I angled our dueling popsicles at each other, Kevin took the photo, and then he went off in search of other prey.

"I've got to hand it to you, Archie," Betty said, taking in the activity around us. "This 'Midsummer Night's Fundraiser' was a great idea."

"Thanks. But, honestly, we should've called it a 'Desperate Times Call for Desperate Measures' fundraiser." I cast a look over the crowded community center, people picking at refreshments, dancing to music, talking. "We're kind of on the ropes, and it was this, or . . ."

Only I didn't know what came after "or." We needed new donors, and an open-invitation party meant to show off the center at its best was the only idea that had come to mind. Munroe was off at his college orientation in Indiana for a few days, so Betty was helping me keep an eye on things, and Kevin was our unofficial photographer.

"It's smart—and fun, too." Betty faced me with an optimistic look. "You're really good at this, you know? You've got an instinct for it, Archie. This is something you should be proud of."

I was trying to think up a way to brush the compliment off when the door to the community center flew open, and Eddie hurtled inside, his eyes wide with panic. "Archie! You gotta come quick—it's Malcolm!"

The sight that greeted us all as we tumbled out into Sketch Alley was shocking. Malcolm Moore, Munroe's kid brother, was bent over a squad car—pinned by some sheriff's deputy I'd never seen before. The name on the guy's lapel was Rayburn, and he was smirking as he declared, "Malcolm Moore, you're under arrest for the attempted murder of Laurence Loomis."

"I didn't do anything!" Malcolm's face was contorted in pain. "I don't even know who that is!"

"You have the right to remain silent," Deputy Rayburn recited loudly, twisting Malcolm's arm behind his back and making the kid cry out. "Anything you say can and will be used against you in a court of law."

There was another deputy there, too, a younger, toothpaste-ad-looking guy with the name Huxley on his lapel, but he wasn't doing anything. His partner was roughing up a minor, and this jerk was just standing around like he didn't want to get his perfect hair mussed.

Malcolm's fate flashed before my eyes, one bad break too many for a kid who'd had nothing *but* bad breaks. Starting forward, I shouted, "Hey, man, watch it—you're hurting him!"

Betty got in front of me, putting her hands on my chest. "Don't, Archie. You'll only make it worse."

And she was right. Suddenly, Rayburn had something to prove, and he drew out his weapon. "All of you need to back up—that means you, Red!"

"I'll call your grandma," I promised Malcolm over the sound of the irate deputy growling out the rest of the Miranda warning. "And

I'll get my mom. She'll act as your attorney, so don't say a word until she gets to the station house! Not a word!"

Malcolm barely had time to nod before he was hauled off the hood of the car and shoved into the back seat.

∧∧∧

"I never tried to kill anybody!" Less than an hour later, seated in an interview room at the sheriff's office, Malcolm stared up at me and my mom with wide, frightened eyes. "I know I've screwed up before, but I would never do that! Dodger used to make us carry weapons, but I never used mine—not even to threaten someone. You have to believe me!"

"We do believe you, Malcolm." My mom's tone was gentle, but her expression was bulletproof, and I already pitied the deputy that would have to go up against her.

"It's some kind of a mistake," I assured him. "You probably have an alibi, anyway, and this'll be cleared up with a few phone calls. Right?"

I said it as much to convince myself as to comfort Malcolm, but he wasn't having it. "I don't know where I was, because they won't even tell me when it happened!" Tossing out his hands, he looked from me to my mom. "But it doesn't matter. I mean, who do I have to back me up? Munroe? Grandma? The deputies won't believe anything they say, and they won't believe anyone from the center, either."

"Let's cross that bridge when we come to it, okay?" My mom sat down in the chair next to Malcolm and put her hand on his shoulder. "Just breathe—you can't afford to lose your cool under questioning. Right now, I'm more concerned about this weapon you mentioned. Can you tell me about it?"

"It was a knife," Malcolm answered miserably, and I shared a worried glance with Mom over his head. "Dodger made us all carry switchblades, 'just in case.' But Munroe and I got rid of it after Archie chased him out of Sketch Alley, I swear!"

"We believe you," Mom repeated firmly.

Looking up at me with stricken eyes, Malcolm asked, "Are you gonna tell my brother about this?"

"You know I can't keep it from him." I shuffled my feet.

"I just . . . I just want Munroe to be proud of me," Malcolm whispered, his eyes shining. "You don't even know half of what we've been through, and now he's got this big chance with Notre Dame, and I . . . I don't want to hold him back."

"You won't." I was emphatic. "This is all a big mistake, and you're gonna be okay—and your brother will *always* be proud of you."

It was just then that the door to the interview room opened, and Tom Keller appeared. "Archie? The deputies are ready to question Malcolm, and I'm afraid you can't be in here. Why don't you come back to my office?"

"Go ahead," my mom said with a nod. And then, to the sheriff, "Tom, maybe after this you and I can have a chat in your office, too. We can talk about how Malcolm's arrest was handled, or how Black youth on the Southside are nearly twice as likely to be stopped by deputies than their white counterparts?"

"We can do that." Sheriff Keller nodded. "Come on, Archie."

∧∧∧

I wasn't going to wait for my mom to plead Malcolm's case. As soon as we were back in Sheriff Keller's office, I launched into a speech defending my friend's brother until Mr. Keller held up his hands in supplication.

"Believe me, Archie, this isn't about character judgments," he'd replied. "It's about evidence. And . . . well, look, Malcolm has a record."

"So what?" I slapped my hands on his desk. The booking room had been packed with a group of drunks brought in for starting a bar brawl, and we could still hear the occasional outburst coming from them. "Half the kids at the center have records—*I* have a record. How come I get a second chance and Malcolm doesn't? The whole reason Munroe and I opened the center in the first place was to give the kids on the Southside a safe space and a few more choices in life."

"Which is a noble goal, and you know how much I respect it." Sheriff Keller sighed. "But Malcolm has also been in trouble for drug-related offenses. We can't just ignore that."

"He moved jingle jangle and Fizzle Rocks for Dodger, because he didn't want his family to be targeted if he refused! He didn't have a choice," I pointed out angrily. "But he's not a drug dealer! And he's never committed a violent crime."

The sheriff rubbed his jaw, looking miserable—as unhappy as I was. "There's also the issue of the knife, Archie. The guy who stabbed Loomis and ran off with two thousand dollars in cash left his knife behind. And it's got Malcolm's fingerprints on it."

"The kid identified the weapon as his property, too." A smug voice came from the doorway, and I snapped around to see Deputy Huxley. He stood there, a cardboard box with LOOMIS scrawled on it tucked in the crook of his left arm; in his right hand, he held a plastic evidence bag containing a switchblade. "Just blurted it right out, before that crooked lawyer of his could shut him up."

"My mom's not crooked!" I exclaimed, but my blood went a little cold just the same. "And so what if it was his knife? That's circumstantial—plus I know for a fact that Munroe made Malcolm get rid of any weapons Dodger gave him months ago. How many *other* prints did you find on that knife?"

"Archie, just let us do our jobs, okay? I promise you, nobody's getting railroaded on my watch." Sheriff Keller was practically begging me, but even as that Huxley guy tossed the knife into the cardboard box and replaced the lid, I could see the satisfaction on his face.

"I'm taking this stuff back to the evidence locker now, Sheriff," the deputy reported in the most butt-kissing tone I'd ever heard.

"But you should know that this kid here tried to interfere with our arrest."

Turning to Sheriff Keller, I snapped, "You should also know that Deputy Huxley's partner used excessive force subduing a minor. I'm not the only witness who will testify that that Rayburn guy tried to break Malcolm's arm tonight!"

"Like anybody would take you seriously!" Huxley stormed into the office, slamming the box of evidence down on a chair. "Everybody in the sheriff's office has your number, Andrews. We all know about Shadow Lake and your time in juvie, and what kind of troublemakers you've recruited for your 'community center.' As far as most of this office is concerned, you're still a lowlife—and obviously your little gang will say whatever you tell them to."

"My 'gang' includes Betty and Kevin," I noted for Sheriff Keller, my jaw stiff. "And I resent the accusation."

With a placating gesture, Sheriff Keller started, "Nobody's being accused of—"

"Personally, I think it's way past time we took a good look at the facts," Huxley blazed on. "A punk who went to juvie on a murder rap—and *broke out*—has established his headquarters in the worst neighborhood in town. Just like Dodger Dickenson."

"That's it!" I shot to my feet, ready to start swinging. "I'm done putting up with insults from this clown-school dropout! Crime rates have gone down in Sketch Alley, thanks to the community center, and you and your partner should *both* lose your badges for what you did tonight!"

Huxley was just as fast. "Listen, Freckles, any time you wanna go—"

"Stop this, right now!" Sheriff Keller was between us in an instant. "Knock it off, the both of you, or I'm—"

"Sheriff?" We were interrupted again—another deputy appearing in the doorway like a magic trick. "We got a situation in the booking room, and it's pretty bad. Those boozers started fighting again, and now it's a total free-for-all. We could use your help."

"And to think I *wanted* this job back," Sheriff Keller groaned, and then he snapped his fingers. "Huxley, you're with me. Archie, stay put—we'll finish this conversation later. One fire at a time."

And with that, they left me in the office—all alone, standing before a box marked loomis that held the one damning piece of evidence against Munroe's little brother.

I didn't let myself think about what I was doing as I lifted the lid, snatched out the bagged switchblade from among the other clutter inside, and jammed it into my waistband.

I knew Malcolm was innocent. Even if I hadn't known he'd disposed of his knife back in the winter, even if it turned out he had no alibi for this Loomis character's mugging, I would never believe he was guilty. One thing I *did* believe? That as long as cops like Rayburn and Huxley were calling the shots, Munroe's brother would never get a fair shake.

Huxley had been taking the box to the evidence locker, which meant they were done with it for the day. Who knew how long it could be before they went looking for the weapon again? It had already been printed and identified . . . it could be weeks before they needed it—before they found out that they no longer had possession of their only clue tying an innocent kid to a serious crime.

I walked back down the hall, hands in my pockets, eyes on the floor. No one stopped me as I scurried through the front room, breaking into a run when I reached the sidewalk. My heart was clanging like a church bell, sweat coursing down my back, and I just kept repeating to myself that I'd done the right thing.

I'd done the right thing.

Hadn't I?

∧∧∧

The great, twisted irony of it all is that Malcolm's innocence was proven a week later, and it was no thanks to me and what I'd "stolen out from under the sheriff's nose." A witness came forward a few days after Malcolm's arrest, implicating a former Ghoulie . . . who admitted his guilt when he was brought in for questioning.

By the time Munroe returned from Notre Dame, everything was already back to normal. His brother's name had been cleared, Laurence Loomis (whoever he was) had recovered from his injuries, and Senator Pendergast had used the incident to springboard his anti-crime campaign into the spotlight. The case was closed, thanks to the guilty party's confession, and the evidence against Malcolm was irrelevant.

I'd never needed to take that knife. If I'd just waited, everything would have worked out, anyway. But I did what I did, and you can't un-ring a bell.

Or so they say.

Poison Pen clearly knew that we'd believed otherwise.

CHAPTER TWENTY

On the night of July Fourth, the rolling green grasses of Pickens Park had been jammed, and everywhere I looked I saw smiling faces—illuminated by the golden glow of handheld sparklers, pressed close for selfies, or aimed upward in anticipation. The air had carried the scents of gunpowder and grilled meat and the lively music of John Philip Sousa.

I'd been there so people could see me enjoying the fireworks.

Today, the park was empty but for a few kids scampering back and forth, parents trailing behind them in the dismal August heat. I'd walked there on autopilot after reading Poison Pen's letter, and I had been sitting on a bench for a long time, staring at the empty gazebo without seeing anything.

I had no idea what to do. No one had seen me take that knife, I was certain of it, and I'd made sure that only a handful of people had learned about it after the fact. So how had Poison Pen found out? Who *could* know, if not someone who'd agreed to share the secret, to take on a risk that might sink them, too? *"I'll make sure it goes down with all hands on deck."*

Who else knew besides those who would never, *could* never, tell?

"You look as if you've seen a ghost, Archiekins."

Glancing up, it was like surfacing from a dream, reality jumping back into focus. "Ronnie?"

"In the flesh." She smiled. She was beautiful, as always, in a flowery halter dress and a wide-brimmed hat to keep the sun off her bare shoulders. "And the sweat. I swear there's more moisture in the air today than in Sweetwater River—clearly I picked the wrong afternoon to go for a walk. Without a life jacket, at any rate."

"Do you want to sit down?" I offered because it was polite. But, secretly, I sort of hoped she'd say no. Not because we were on bad terms, but because it still sometimes felt awkward and disappointing not to be what we once were.

And also because I wasn't sure how I was going to avoid blurting out what was on my mind if she hung around. Ronnie knew me about as well as I knew myself, and there wasn't much I could keep from her. For a long time, she was the first person I turned to in times of trouble, but this was something I couldn't share. *"If you tell anyone about this letter . . . I'll make you regret it."*

Another cruel twist of fate, since she was one of six other people who were already involved—whether she knew it or not.

For a moment, it looked as if she would say no and spare us

both an awkward moment, but then her smile softened. "Actually, I'd like that. It feels as if we've barely seen one another since the school year ended."

"And now you're getting ready to start a new year at a new school." I offered a smile that I hoped came across more natural than it felt.

"Life at Barnard draws nigh." She settled beside me, a trace of her perfume drifting on the humid breeze, and something twinged just below my heart. "And please don't misunderstand me, because I won't be leaving without regrets, but I cannot wait to decamp from Riverdale."

I knew what she meant, and yet I flinched at the way it sounded. "Have things really been that bad here for you?"

"Honestly, Archie? They've been *worse*." The look she wore was one of surprise. "Disregarding just the epic power struggles I've had with my parents alone—both of whom have served this city as mayor, need I remind—since moving here I've never had to so consistently fear for my life. And then there's—" But she stopped herself. With another fleeting smile, she concluded, "I'm sorry. I know how much Riverdale means to you. But it's hard to escape the fact that I moved here because my life fell apart, and I've been fighting to piece it back together ever since."

"I get it," I said. "But you had happy moments here, too, right?"

"Of *course* I did." Reaching over, she put her hand on mine, and I tensed all over. At the moment, being reminded of all the things we'd had and lost only made it harder to keep from telling her about Poison Pen. "No matter how I feel about this place, I will *always* be grateful for you—for *us*. That will never change. No matter what happens, you'll always be my Archiekins."

"And you can still call me when you finally realize New York is too crowded and noisy and filled with pizza rats to live in," I volleyed, trying to make a joke out of a sad moment. "Like it or not, you're one of us now, Veronica Lodge. Part of you belongs in Riverdale."

With a peal of laughter, she said, "Fear not, stalwart one. New York is most assuredly both the best and worst place on earth. Give me four weeks of MTA breakdowns, inconsiderate tourists, and unsanitary bathrooms, and I'll wax nostalgic about the time I threw a Molotov cocktail at a serial killer in La Bonne Nuit."

I laughed a little, too, turning back to the gazebo, trying not to think about what my days were going to be like in just a few weeks without Veronica. Or Betty or Jughead. Or Cheryl, Reggie, Kevin, and Munroe. I'd never been a great student, but I'd never really worried about the impact that would have on my future, either—because I'd always seen my future *here*.

Since I was old enough to understand what a future was, my dad had been my personal hero. He always seemed bigger than anybody else, able to do anything; he could replace car parts, unclog a drainpipe, rewire a light switch, explain why the dino-saurs died. He'd made a great life, right here in his hometown. Even when following my mom's path became clearly out of my reach, I always knew I could follow *his* and still be happy.

Thanks to my dad, at least partly, I'd always thought that being an Andrews meant being part of Riverdale—that my family and this town shared DNA. But what if I was wrong? What if my future was nothing like I had ever imagined it to be?

Eager to change the subject, I coughed. "I heard about what happened Saturday night. I'm really—"

"It was certainly quite the scandal," she interrupted quickly. "If nothing else, life in Riverdale has never been boring. Oh, and you'll adore this: During his speech to the guests, Senator Pendergast declared that Huxley had *personally* apprehended the mugger who stabbed Laurence Loomis." Shaking her head with disgust, she added, "And even though everyone in the room knew it was a total crock, because the *real* culprit con-fessed to Sheriff Keller a week later, they all clapped and smiled, anyway."

"It's still pretty wild that someone hacked into your laptop and altered that slideshow," I commented. "Who do you think was responsible?"

"I . . . I don't really know, and to tell the truth, Archie, it's all something I'd prefer to forget about." Her tone was so abrupt and so firm that it startled me. "It was a profoundly unpleasant evening. I hope you understand?"

"Yeah, sure, of course." I gave a nod, and for a moment, relative silence reigned over Pickens Park. Those frolicking children were running out of steam in the punishing heat, and the only sound to be heard was the ebb and flow of droning cicadas.

Then, before I could figure out how to say something without saying everything, she blurted, "What would you do if you had a secret—a dangerous one—that could hurt the people you cared about, and yet for certain reasons you couldn't tell a soul?"

Ice-cold prickles danced all the way up my spine and across my scalp. Frozen in place, I asked, "What do you mean, Ronnie? Exactly."

"I don't mean anything—it's just a—a hypothetical." Her cheeks turned pink. "Obviously, if I were being serious . . . Archie, if I were being serious, I couldn't tell you. *I couldn't tell a soul.* Because of what might happen."

I stared at her, wishing I could read her thoughts—wishing she could read mine. "Because someone might be watching?"

"Archie . . ." she murmured, her lips barely moving—but her spine was stiff as a rail, and I could at least read her body language.

"Ronnie . . . have you gotten any special mail recently?"

"Stop." She turned a look on me that was alive with fear. "Don't ask about that, Archie. Because someone *is* watching. Always. If what you're talking about is what I think you're talking about, all I can tell you is that it's no joke. Whatever

you think, whatever it is you're afraid they'll do, they *will*—and worse."

Flicking a glance around the park, all I saw were those tiring kids and their exhausted parents . . . but suddenly I felt Poison Pen's eyes on me like a spotlight. Leaning closer, whispering lower, I exclaimed, "But it isn't possible! Who would do something like this, and how could they have—"

"Archie, don't!" Ronnie shot to her feet, knuckles white around the clutch purse in her hands. "Don't ask me those questions—don't ask them at all! And please don't try to be a hero. This person . . . you have no idea what they're capable of. We could both end up at the bottom of the river or . . . or flattened by a bus, just for having this conversation!" Leaning closer, she hissed, "This person, *PP*, knows things they shouldn't know. They have access to private conversations and traffic camera feeds and . . . and who knows what else!"

"Ronnie—"

"I'm sorry, Archie. I'm so sorry, but . . . you're on your own." Thoroughly spooked, Veronica backed away, her posture rigid and her mouth tight. "Whatever *PP* is asking you to do? Do it. Just do it, and pray that your friends will forgive you."

And, with that, she was gone.

For a while, I just stayed there in the park—staring at the gazebo, listening to the cicadas, and wondering who might be watching me. Ronnie's words kept clanging around in my head, making the same problems I'd had all along seem somehow even worse. It had been a while since I'd seen her so paranoid about something that didn't involve her parents, with their endless scheming and bottomless resources.

Hiram Lodge had bought half the city, covered up crimes, and connived his way into the mayor's office. He'd used his influence to frame me for murder, to sabotage his daughter's businesses, to change the laws to enable his own pursuit of more power. An instinctive part of me wanted to believe that this was yet another one of his plots.

But anonymous letters and veiled threats weren't his style. He liked to sneak up on his victims, sure, but when he struck, he wanted you to know who was dealing the blow. Psychological harassment using a cutesy pseudonym was definitely not his typical MO.

A bird swooped low, emitting a sharp cry that almost sent me out of my skin. Heart pounding, I cast another instinctive look around the park, but I saw nothing. *Nothing.* Even the kids were gone by now. I was alone . . . and yet it still felt like I was under surveillance.

If not Hiram Lodge, then who could possibly be able to access traffic cameras, to spy on people and eavesdrop? Who could have learned that I stole that switchblade on June 23, when I knew for a solid fact that it had never even been noticed missing?

Who could have known—and who could have possibly cared? Laurence Loomis had recovered, and no matter how he felt about the way his attack was handled by the sheriff's office, they ultimately got a confession out of the perpetrator. Justice had been done. The only people I could even imagine feeling cheated were Rayburn and Huxley, whose moment of glory was lost when their big arrest was revealed to be a big mistake.

But the deputies weren't the only ones using Malcolm's arrest to boost their image, I realized. *"Senator Pendergast declared that Huxley had* personally *apprehended the mugger who stabbed Laurence Loomis."* It was a bald-faced lie but certainly preferable to the truth—that Pendergast had been crowing publicly over a bad arrest.

In fact, for a full week after it happened, the senator had bragged to reporters about how quickly the sheriff's office had caught the bad guy in the Loomis case. He must have been pretty angry about all the egg on his face when the truth came out. While the community center was keeping disadvantaged youth off the streets, it was also lowering arrest rates—and even if that made the sheriff happy, it had to annoy Pendergast, who needed full jail cells to prove how "tough on crime" he was. The wannabe governor had embarrassed himself pretty badly by publicly declaring Malcolm guilty before all the facts had come to light.

As another thought struck, a rush of excitement swept through me, and I sat up straighter on the bench. Patrick Pendergast—PP—*Poison Pen*? Like Mr. Lodge, he was one of few people who might actually care about what I'd done, and he had the resources to uncover the rest. Who knew what sort of information he had access to through Huxley, or how much he could buy with bribes and spies and listening devices?

Okay, maybe I couldn't fill in all the blanks—like why he would do all *this* instead of just turning us in—but this was Riverdale, and way less explainable stuff had turned out to be true. Plus, if Ronnie thought *her* Saturday night was bad, Pendergast's had been infinitely worse, and he'd followed up one campaign-rocking scandal with another, only a few days later. Maybe he'd simply cracked under the stress.

With a jolt, it hit me: Clearly, Veronica had received hate mail from Poison Pen as well. And while I had no idea what her letter might have said, it couldn't be a coincidence that she'd been made a target *the same week that she'd publicly embarrassed Senator Pendergast.*

Jumping to my feet, I did a 360, but the park was still empty. Now even the birds were silent, the trees drooping under the ruthless sun. But for the first time since I opened that letter, I felt invigorated, and I started walking at a pace just shy of a jog.

If I was going to expose a senator, I needed to plan—and I didn't have much time.

CHAPTER TWENTY-ONE

Back at home, I changed my clothes four times. First, into my best suit—okay, my *only* suit—because it seemed like the appropriate thing to wear to scam my way into a state senator's office. But the suit made me think of my dad's funeral, and I couldn't bear it, so I changed back into my T-shirt and shorts. If Pendergast was behind this, then he already knew enough about me that dressy clothes weren't going to fool him.

But then I could hear one of my mom's lectures, echoing from the past, telling me all about how quickly juries judge people based on their appearance. During my murder trial, what I wore every day was planned out as carefully as our opening and closing statements. So I put on a polo shirt and a pair of khakis, like a Stonewall Prep kid on Casual Friday, and then stared in the mirror for about fifteen minutes trying not to punch my own reflection.

In the end, I changed back into my T-shirt and shorts and got in the car.

It was the moments like this that made me miss Jughead the most. Going to confront a power-hungry politician about being the possible author of anonymous threats was way more in his wheelhouse than mine. The whole drive, I kept asking myself what he would say in my shoes—but then I'd get flustered and angry when trying to rehearse my answers.

I was on my own. Jug wasn't speaking to me and Ronnie wanted to stay as far away from Poison Pen as possible. Who else could I turn to? Betty was the only other person I'd want by my side, but could I risk bringing her into this? If Pendergast *was* the one who'd written that letter, we could confront him, get our answers, and settle things; but if I was wrong . . .

"Whatever you think, whatever it is you're afraid they'll do, they will—and worse."

If I was wrong, I had no right asking Betty to put herself in more danger on my behalf. Not after everything she'd already done.

According to his website, Pendergast had an office in downtown Riverdale—a tiny storefront space between a barbershop and a café. When I arrived, I pulled my car to the curb and sat, staring at the opaque glass door, beginning to realize just how in over my head I was. I didn't even know if he would be in. Aside from this location, he had another office upstate, as well as dozens of spaces across the state he'd rented out to coordinate his campaign. But for all I knew, he could be golfing today. In Scotland.

Besides, even if he *was* at this particular office, I still didn't know how to talk my way into his private chambers—or what

I'd say if I got there. Hands on the wheel, my brain spinning helplessly, I just sat there in the car for long minutes.

And then my phone buzzed.

Unknown ID:

> I guess you and Ronnie must have had a pretty productive conversation. I'm truly fascinated to know what you think you're going to do at Senator Pendergast's office. Whatever it is, though, it's sure to be boneheaded and poorly planned, and I am very tempted to let you go through with it! But, sadly, for your own good, I think I need to keep you from throwing yourself on yet another grenade.

Unknown ID:

> See, you're never the grenade's only casualty. (Over the years, you've caused more collateral damage than a drunken steam shovel operator!) But it never stops you from trying. And just now, there's too great a chance you'll blurt out everything and spoil my fun by landing all of your little friends behind bars. So permit me to save you from yourself this time, Archie Andrews. Stop now, before you do something everyone will regret.

I'm not who you think I am . . . but I'm just as dangerous. The ONLY reason I'm still keeping your secrets is because there's something I want you to do. Say yes, and nobody else ever has to know what you and your friends did. Say no, and . . . Well, I seriously suggest that you say yes. Now pay attention, because you'll need to memorize and repeat the following message.

When I saw what Poison Pen expected me to do, my heart hit the ground like that asteroid in *Deep Impact*. At first, I wrote back and refused, point blank, and then images started appearing on my phone, one after another. Ronnie wrecking her own car; Toni and Jug in Greendale; Kevin kissing Deputy Huxley; Cheryl driving the stolen car. And, finally, a very familiar figure in a black hood—racing down the alley beside the sheriff's station.

With all these puzzle pieces in hand, Sheriff Keller would have no trouble deducing the whole story, and with the pressure coming down on his office, he'd have no choice but to throw the book at us as hard as he could.

The choice before me was unthinkable . . . but in the end, it was no choice at all. *"Just do it, and pray that your friends will forgive you."* My hands cold and my face hot, I sat in my car for another hour, memorizing a speech for a terrible command performance.

CHAPTER TWENTY-TWO

The bell over the door at Pop's jingled, and I flinched like I'd heard a gunshot. Another one, I mean—my track record of bloodshed and misery at the Chock'Lit Shoppe was undefeated. But I kept my eyes on the mug of coffee in my hands, the dark liquid going cold. I couldn't bear to look up, to see my fate coming.

"Archie?" The voice, bright and friendly, was a spear in my chest. "I got your message. I mean, obviously, I got your message—here I am." Dropping onto the bench across from me, Betty flashed a curious smile. She was tanned from a summer spent outdoors, looking as close to relaxed as I think any of us could possibly feel after the year we'd all had. "Why did you want to meet me here? And . . . why wouldn't you say over text?"

"It's just . . ." My throat swelled, the single sip of coffee I'd managed to swallow now burning my stomach. "There was something I needed to tell you, and I . . . it's better if I do it in person."

"Okay." Her smile faltered, but held. "That's a little . . . ominous. What's going on?"

"Um, summer is ending soon, and we're all kind of going separate ways, so . . ." I forced myself to look her in the eye, because if I was going to go through with this, I didn't deserve to avoid how painful it would be. "What I'm trying to tell you is that I'm glad we won't see each other anymore, Betty."

Whatever she thought I was going to say, that wasn't it. Her smile dying off, she blinked. "Wait . . . what?"

"I never had the guts to admit it before, but . . . I've always been scared of you."

She drew back from the edge of the table. "Archie, what are you saying?"

"Even before we knew you had an actual murderer's blood in your veins, that you were part serial killer, I was afraid living next door to you," I barreled ahead, my face hot, acid stinging the back of my throat. "I used to have nightmares about you climbing through my bedroom window at night and slitting my throat or something."

"I w-would never hurt you." Her protest was genuine and plaintive, her eyes suddenly shiny, and a part of me crumbled inside. "You know I wouldn't—not ever."

"The truth is . . . the truth is, none of us know what you're capable of. *You* don't know what you're capable of. You've been fighting Dark Betty for years, but she's only getting closer to the surface." I put my hands under the table, squeezing them into fists so tight it hurt. "Maybe it's time you just admitted that Dark Betty has been the real you all along."

Silent tears rolled down Betty's cheeks, and she turned away from me as she swiped at them. In that moment, I hated myself—but I hated Poison Pen even more. *"If you ask me, Betty Cooper is a bad influence on you . . . and I think it's time you told her that to her face."* All these horrible, hurtful statements had been scripted for me, designed to strike at Betty's deepest fears, and they were unforgivable.

"How can you say these things, Archie?" she finally asked in a broken whisper. "After everything we've been through? How can you . . . how could you . . . ?"

Grabbing the item that had been sitting next to me, I placed it on the table in front of her. It was the framed photo of us from the midsummer fundraising party, our Popsicles crossed, our expressions goofy and lighthearted. "Here—I didn't want this when you gave it to me, and I definitely won't hold on to it after you leave."

Some emotion swam across Betty's face, confusion darting swiftly in and out of her eyes. "But you w—"

"I hope you can figure out how to keep your darkness under control." I lunged to my feet. There was no way I'd be able to stick around even a second longer than it took to finish my lines. "But I'm done being part of the struggle. We're moving in different directions, and that's a good thing. Once you leave for Yale, don't bother to stay in touch."

Unable to speak another word, I turned on my heel and stalked out of the Chock'Lit Shoppe, a chorus of startled faces watching me go. I'd been loud enough to be overheard, because those were my instructions, and I wanted desperately to believe that Poison Pen had been in the diner with us. I wanted to grab each and every person there by the shirtfront, to shake them until I got a confession. But instead I just marched to my car and yanked open the door.

Because the truth was, even if the things Poison Pen said to me were cruel? They were also right. Far too many people had gotten hurt as a result of my careless, unthinking attempts to make something of myself—to prove my courage, to do the right thing. Betty was just the latest in a long, undeserving line of innocent bystanders getting hit by the flack.

The latest, and the last. I was done playing hero. For good.

In my last glimpse of the Chock'Lit Shoppe before I swung the car around and drove off, I saw Betty's tear-streaked face in the window—watching me leave.

Oh, I know what you're thinking: Poor Betty Cooper. Why did she have to get hurt when Archie is the one who did something wrong? Well, let me tell you something. <u>THEY ALL DID SOMETHING WRONG</u>. All of them deserve to be hurt!

Archie is not the victim! Betty is not the victim! <u>I AM THE VICTIM</u>.

They would love for you to believe their sob stories, but there are people in Riverdale who suffer way more than they do. If anything, they've had it <u>easy</u> all these years—inviting disaster and challenging killers, then throwing other people's bodies between themselves and the worst dangers imaginable.

How many corpses piled up thanks to Penelope Blossom, the Gargoyle King? How many lives have been destroyed in Hiram Lodge's bottomless thirst for dominance? How many people did Hal Cooper kill to rid Riverdale of "sin"?

Jason Blossom, Geraldine Grundy, Midge Klump, Dilton Doiley, Ben Button, Joaquin DeSantos, Cassidy Bullock and his friends . . . they're all dead.

And yet the "Core Four" and their band of insufferable sidekicks keep marching on. The road to Riverdale is paved with good intentions.

Here's the truth: Archie never deserved Betty.

She's always been the brains of his operation. She's always been the one to step in when he's screwed up—and, my goodness, has she stepped on one rake after another on his behalf! He finally needs to learn what it's like when the chips are really down and there's no one there to help you pick them up. He needs to know what it feels like when everyone you're supposed to count on in your time of need is gone and you have to face the worst alone. Like I did.

No more Veronica pulling strings, no more Jughead playing wingman, no more Betty fixing his problems.

Of course, Miss Cooper has her own crimes to answer for—and that's where all this has been leading. Archie may be the reason all these targets are falling, but Betty was the one who set them up in the first place. And it's finally time for her to learn my name.

Five down and one to go, and I've saved the biggest bang for last.

—Poison Pen

PART SIX
BETTY COOPER
THURSDAY

CHAPTER TWENTY-THREE

As pretty much everyone in Riverdale knows, there was a time when a mysterious text from Archie saying that he "needed to tell me something important" would have filled me with glee. I might have even practiced my "delighted surprise" face so that when he told me he'd been secretly, madly in love with me for years, I could deliver the perfect reaction.

Well. That time was long ago. Even if Archie and I had a few . . . let's call them "close moments" this past year, I'm no longer the starry-eyed girl I once was, and I don't have the same illusions I used to—about either love or the boy next door.

I know myself better than I did back then. I have bigger goals, a sense of who I am and what I deserve, and I know what kind of sacrifices are worth making to see my dreams come true.

I also know Archie better. Even I have to admit that I was a little pathetic freshman year, following him around and waiting for him to see me. If I noticed his flaws, I found reasons to ignore them or justify them. And when I finally stopped looking at him through rose-colored glasses, I realized that some of the things I liked about him weren't even real.

Which isn't to say Archie Andrews is unimpressive! He's still handsome, dependable, loyal, courageous, and full of integrity. He's also one of the most compassionate people I've ever met.

Or so I thought.

When I showed up at Pop's yesterday to find out what important thing he "needed to tell me" face-to-face, he proceeded to spit out some of the most hurtful things that anyone has ever said to me. And, to make it worse, he knew exactly what he was doing. His words . . . they were personal and deliberate, and he said them knowing just how deeply they would wound me.

Never in my wildest fantasies had I ever imagined that Archie Andrews could be capable of such cruelty.

But one thing he did was strange. (Well, stranger than the fact that he did any of it at all.) Handing me that framed photo from his desk at the community center, the one of us at the fundraiser earlier this summer, he said, *"I didn't want this when you gave it to me."*

Only, the thing is: I didn't give him that photo.

After the party ended, Kevin plugged his camera's memory card directly into Archie's laptop and uploaded all the photos he'd taken. Archie himself printed them out, putting the best ones up in his office or on the walls around the center. I'd been so touched the first time I saw the framed snapshot above his desk, and I'd kind of made a big deal out of it.

There was no way he'd forgotten where it originally came from.

So I guess you could say I went into Nancy Drew mode on the spot. The minute I got home, I took the backing off the frame (because unless the picture itself was a message, there was pretty much only one place a possible clue could be hidden), and I found two notes tucked inside. Folded down into neat squares, one had my name on it, and the other had Archie's.

And when I read them, a lot of the strange things that had been happening in Riverdale this week began to make complete sense.

∿∿∿

Betty—

I guess if you're reading this, it means you figured out that I was trying to tell you something by giving you our picture. And I hope it also means that I didn't get caught doing it. (By the way, I seriously hope you waited until you were in a private place before taking the frame apart, because the person watching me seems to have eyes everywhere.)

First, I'm so sorry for everything I said to you. You have to know I didn't mean any of it, but if I didn't say that stuff, everything that happened on July Fourth (and everything that led up to it) would have come out. I'm being blackmailed by someone who knows exactly what went down this summer, and they have the kind of proof that would ruin all our lives if it got into Sheriff Keller's hands. (Photos—of almost everyone.)

You're the smartest person I know, Betty. If anyone can figure out who's behind this and why they're doing it, it's you. The other note I'm hiding in the picture frame is the one I got from the blackmailer, so you can see what we're dealing with. Whoever this person is, they call themselves "Poison Pen."

Good luck, and I'm sorry. Again.

—Archie

∿∿∿

By the time I reached the end of Archie's message, even before I picked up the note that accompanied it, I was already beginning to understand some things. It wasn't my first encounter with Poison Pen's handiwork—I'd seen exactly what they threatened Veronica with last weekend, and I was pretty sure what they had made her do to keep it hidden.

V "accidentally" exposing Pendergast's affair in the middle

of his daughter's engagement party, Juggie abruptly ending his oldest and most important friendship, Kevin's sudden moral quandary about his role in what happened on July Fourth, Cheryl's secret confession video, Archie's speech. All week, strange things had been happening.

Apparently, the culprit hadn't been Penelope Blossom, after all. But who, then? Veronica had been right, that afternoon at the library: Without knowing more, the list of potential suspects was almost too long to be worth compiling. But, then again, I did know something now that we didn't just a few days ago.

When V and I discussed her letter, we'd both believed—because we had no reason to think otherwise—that it was about *her*. That she was being singled out by someone who had witnessed her act of vandalism and wanted to mess with her. But the picture that Archie had helped me start piecing together looked very different.

Who could have known what we did? And who could possibly have come up with actual evidence, when we were all so careful to avoid being seen? Veronica had even dismantled the security camera in the parking garage before she wrecked her car . . . so where had photos of her come from? And why were the notes so *personal?*

Lastly, and perhaps most intriguing: Why had Poison Pen forced both Veronica and Kevin (if I was right about Kevin) to do something that hurt the Pendergasts, specifically?

The letters I'd seen weren't just taunting—they were filled with a gloating sadism. Whoever Poison Pen was, they were *angry*, and they wanted us to hurt. I knew Archie well enough to know that it would have caused him real anguish, being made to say those things to me. But that scene we'd played out at the Chock'Lit Shoppe had been written to punish *both* of us.

"Elizabeth?" My mother's voice broke through my thoughts, her footsteps approaching quickly along the hall, and I hastily slid the two notes under my laptop just as she burst into my room. "Oh, there you are."

"Yup. In my room." I gestured around, a practiced smile on my face. "I actually spend a lot of time here—and often with the door closed! On purpose."

"You know how I feel about closed doors in this house." Mom cocked an authoritarian brow.

"I know how you feel about boundaries in general," I muttered. But I didn't really want to rehash this old argument with my mother. After everything that happened while she was in Edgar Evernever's thrall, she'd actually made a huge effort to strengthen our relationship. There'd been a few . . . setbacks, but there was more trust between us now than there used to be. "Why were you looking for me?"

"There was a letter for you in the mailbox." She thrust it out to me. "No return address, but it looks fancy. Maybe someone's going-away party? Veronica must be leaving for Barnard soon, and heaven knows that girl can't do a single thing without some ridiculous fanfare—"

"Mom." I cut her off in a mildly warning tone, and she shut her mouth.

"You're right, you're right." Tossing her hands up, she sighed. "Veronica is your friend, and she's been a good one. For the most part. Even if she has taken advantage of you, and her father is a criminal kingpin, and she—"

"*Mom.*" I glared a silent reminder of the metaphorical glass house we lived in when it came to taking the sins of someone's father into consideration.

This time, my mom just gave an obedient nod and mimicked zipping her lips shut. With a little wave, she backed out into the hall and shut the door behind her. Progress.

Which left me alone, sitting by the window, with a white square envelope that had no return address—the rear flap sealed with a red wax roundel bearing a monogrammed *PP*. It took approximately zero Nancy Drew-ing to understand what had come for me at last, but I still held my breath as I drew the letter out.

∿∿

Dear Betty,

I've never understood why people describe you as "the girl next door," but then, Lizzie Borden also lived next door to someone, didn't she? So maybe it's accurate after all.

Following a devastating breakup (be it friend or otherwise), most people drown their sorrows in ice cream and binge-watching sad movies—but you? For all I know, the Black Hood's daughter finds comfort in the torture of small animals, or planning how she'll arrange the bodies she's going to someday bury in her future crawl space.

Or maybe, Betty, you're just devising another meticulously plotted crime that will demand the complicity of each and every one of your friends. (And I know you saw that letter I wrote to Veronica, so I won't beat around the bush.)

On the night of July Fourth, you broke into the evidence locker at the Rockland County Sheriff's Office in order to return the switchblade that Archie stole.

Just imagine the ramifications if it were made known that someone breached the evidence locker without getting caught! All it would take is one halfway decent lawyer to Erin Brockovich the county, and every single active investigation would be cast into terminal doubt due to possible tampering. Rightful convictions would be overturned, guilty men would walk on technicalities ...

including some of your personal enemies.

How do you suppose the admissions board at Yale would react if they learned how smart you <u>really</u> are, Betts? Smart enough to mastermind the successful infiltration of the station house, all to keep your buddy Archie Andrews from facing justice for stealing that knife. You've had such a hard time living down your father's reputation—how hard will it be to live down your own?

I'll get right to it. I want you to write a story about July Fourth for the front page of tomorrow's edition of the <u>Riverdale Register</u>. (And I don't really care what you have to do to get your story <u>on</u> the front page. You're a resourceful girl; you'll figure out a way.) In this article, at least one member of your criminal conspiracy must be <u>fully</u> incriminated.

Archie would fall hard—but maybe he deserves it. Cheryl and Veronica probably have enough money to survive, but they'd hate you forever. Kevin's dad would fight for him, and as for Juggie . . . well, you could always just be a Petty Betty and leave for Connecticut with an ugly good-bye.

Or you can expose yourself and tank the future you worked so hard to save after your father turned you into public poison.

Make a decision soon, hon, because you only have until the <u>Register's</u> master file is sent to the printer tonight. And if you don't do it, I'm exposing <u>all of you</u>.

In the meantime, keep this letter just between us. Ronniekins learned the hard way that when I say to <u>KEEP YOUR MOUTH SHUT OR PAY THE CONSEQUENCES</u>, I really do mean it. Don't make me teach you the same lesson.

I'm watching you.

—Poison Pen

⌄⌄⌄

As I folded the letter closed again, all the air left my lungs, and it felt as if I were being crushed flat. Automatically, I glanced out the window at the sun, already on its descent—and I shivered. *"On the night of July Fourth, you broke into the evidence locker at the Rockland County Sheriff's Office."*

If only that was all I'd done.

CHAPTER TWENTY-FOUR

After the countless miseries I'd endured throughout senior year—manipulations, rejections, and false accusations, learning that people I loved had been hypnotically programmed to kill me—I'd really been looking forward to a mellow summer. One last lazy hurrah of inner tubes down the Sweetwater, concerts in the park, and the return of Riverdale's iconic fireworks display on July Fourth. I'd missed my summer traditions, and all I wanted was to create one farewell memory of my hometown that didn't have terror and corpses in it.

I should have been more specific.

One week before Independence Day, I found myself at Thistlehouse—plotting out a meticulous crime that demanded the complicity of all my friends.

"It has to be the night of the fourth," I'd said, making eye contact with everyone present—Veronica, Jughead, Kevin, Cheryl, Toni, and Archie. The curtains were drawn, the air scented with jasmine and rose. "Most of the town will be gathered in Pickens Park . . . which means a heavy presence by law enforcement."

"She's right." Kevin nodded, worrying his hands together. "The station house will be down to a skeleton crew that night. One deputy on the desk, and two on call. If we're really going to break into the evidence locker, it's pretty much the only opportunity we'll get."

"Understood." Veronica had her eyes on the sheet of notebook paper where I'd sketched out my plan in rudimentary bullet points. "I can call the station and lure the two on-call deputies out. I'll report . . . a burglary, maybe?"

"At the Pembrooke?" Jughead lifted his brows in doubt. "After Cheryl and Toni stole Hermione's Glamergé eggs, security there was tripled. They'd figure out the truth in minutes, and you'd be toast. All of us would be toast."

"Okay . . ." Veronica touched the black pearls that encircled her throat. "What if it was my car? I could smash it up, deface it, make it look like a possible threat against me." She smiled without humor. "Daddy's dragged our family through the mud more than once, but people still jump when they hear the Lodge name. I'll keep them busy as long as I can."

"That still leaves the deputy at the desk," Kevin observed. "I accessed my dad's duty roster, and it must be one of the guys who joined while FP was sheriff, because I don't know the name. Hayes Huxley?"

"Huxley?" Archie practically exploded. "*That* jerk?"

Kevin blinked. "Oh, I take it we have history?"

"He was one of the deputies who arrested Malcolm," I explained. "The one who just stood there and did nothing."

"Wait, *that* was Deputy Huxley?" Kevin's eyes bulged. When all of us cast curious looks in his direction, his cheeks turned pink. Scratching the back of his neck, he murmured, "Okay, this might be my job. I think I can draw him away from his post long enough for you to do . . . whatever."

"Even when he's the only one in the building?" Cheryl was skeptical.

"Maybe *especially* if he's the only one in the building . . . yeah." Kevin cleared his throat.

"We'll need a getaway car," I went on. "Just in case. And if something goes wrong with the plan, or if there's a witness—even a passerby—it can't be a vehicle that could be traced back to any one of us."

"I suspect that's where I come in." Jughead gave me a conspiratorial smirk across the table, and I smiled back. "There's a scrapyard I buy parts from in Greendale, and they always have old cars sitting around. I can boost one, easy . . . but I can't be your driver." He sat back. "Sheriff Keller made a personal appeal to me to involve the Serpents in crowd control at Pickens Park for the fourth. It would be hard to back out now without a decent explanation."

"Actually, I think it's a good idea if you cooperate," I said, thinking. "And, Archie, you should go along as well." He was about to protest, so I cut him off. "Out of all of us, you're the one who'll be most in need of plausible deniability if anything goes wrong."

"I will need a lookout." Jughead cracked his knuckles nervously. "The place I'm thinking of has terrible security, but there's a routine neighborhood patrol, and a risk of being seen."

"I'll do it." Toni spoke up even before the last words had left his mouth. "We've worked together before, and you'll need someone who knows the drill. No offense to everyone here, but . . . none of you have ever committed grand theft auto."

"That *felt* like an insult, even though it didn't *sound* like an insult," Kevin murmured.

"And I shall be your wheelwoman." Cheryl's announcement was peremptory. "I've always wanted to live out my *Baby Driver* fantasy at least once. And, of course, my skills in this particular arena are quite unmatched among those present. I've mastered both automatic and manual transmissions, and if necessary I'm even rated to fly a helicopter. So I'm sure there won't be any objections to my taking this role?"

"Actually, Cheryl, you were just the person I had in mind," I returned smoothly. Although, if I'm honest, that would have been my response no matter which job she'd claimed. It was always best not to argue with her.

"Very well, then." Veronica reached out and put her hands on the table, ticking off each of my bullet points with a tap of her finger. "We know how we'll remove the deputies from the station house, how we'll obtain our getaway vehicle, and who will drive it. All that remains is determining who should break into the evidence locker itself."

"Me." Archie had trouble looking at any of us, his eyes fixed on Veronica's fingers. "I'm the only reason all of you are involved in the first place. The biggest risk should be mine."

"No, Archie." I was prepared for this, and I made my tone just as firm as Cheryl's had been. "We're trying to get you out of trouble—not into more of it. And like I said, out of all of us, you're the one who actually needs to be seen and remembered that night. Besides, this plan is my idea. If anyone is taking the biggest risk, it's me."

Which was how, one week later, I found myself in the passenger seat of a stolen car, idling at the curb outside the Rockland County station house, waiting for Kevin to text the all clear. In one hand, I held the plastic bag containing Malcolm Moore's old switchblade—the sole evidence that linked him to Laurence Loomis's mugging—and in the other I clutched a scrap of familiar black fabric.

When my phone buzzed with a notification (*we're leaving, side entrance*) the suddenness of it made me jump. "Okay, it's time."

"*Bonne chance*, cousin," Cheryl trilled as I reached for the door handle.

"You know, you could just say 'good luck' like a normal person."

"No." She smiled tightly, her crimson lipstick like dried blood. "I couldn't."

On that note, I got out, starting up the sidewalk with fireworks exploding overhead. Just as I reached the walkway to the station house, I tucked the knife in my pocket and pulled that black fabric over my head—a dark hood, with two holes cut out for my eyes.

It was one of very few things from my father that I'd held on to. This particular item he'd led me to discover in the old Conway house, hoping it would awaken some sympathy in me for the Black Hood.

It hadn't worked . . . but even when I'd intended to burn the thing, I'd found myself unable to go through with it.

I don't know why I wore it that night. Maybe because it was convenient, or because the Black Hood was known to have imitators and I figured it would throw off the scent if I was seen. Or maybe it was because, as I committed one of my last criminal acts in Riverdale, I couldn't resist the pull of my father's memory.

Either way, when I shoved through the doors of the sheriff's office, the silence disturbed only by the ringing of the phone at the front desk, it was with my face covered. My eyes scanned the room, but I knew where I was headed. Darting past the front desk, I slipped through an open door and down a hallway, turning twice before I came to the evidence locker.

It was a climate-controlled room guarded by a metal door with an electronic keypad. Kevin had managed to sneak the code off his father's cell phone, and I punched it in with nervous fingers. If the cipher had been changed, all this would be for nothing; I would have to kick Malcolm's switchblade into a corner and hope that when it was discovered, it was quietly returned to its rightful place out of embarrassment. If anyone got suspicious and raised a stink . . . well, we'd done our best to wipe the bag clean of Archie's prints.

But the keypad blipped, the light turned green, and the door unlocked. My blood racing, my skin electrified with excitement, I found the box marked LOOMIS and replaced the switchblade where it belonged. I was back in the hallway seconds later, headed for the front door. The phone at the desk was still ringing, and the sound rubbed my nerves raw. All I wanted was to put this night behind me.

And that's when I received a text from Cheryl's burner phone.

[Blocked 1]:

Change of plans. Company out front. Whatever you're doing, time to wrap it up!

I froze. I was just close enough to the doorway that opened on the lobby that I could see the front window—and the Rockland County sheriff's cruiser pulling to the curb outside. My heart did a series of violent calisthenics in my chest, and I jerked backward. The on-call deputies were still with Veronica, or she would have texted as well . . . so this was someone else. A pair of Riverdale's Finest that had left Pickens Park early for some reason.

Backing farther away down the hall, my own foolish words echoed loudly in my ears. *"This plan is my idea. If anyone is taking the biggest risk . . . it's me."* What an egotist I was, to think I was so smart that the biggest risk would pose no risk at all. I couldn't leave through the back exit—a bay where squad cars were protected by a wraparound fence topped with razor wire. So, firing off a reply to Cheryl, I started for the door to the alley.

But when I crashed out into the night, sprinting for the getaway car, even though I knew Huxley would see me, I didn't expect the gunshots that followed.

The bullets missed, and our escape was clean (well, mostly . . .
there was the issue of the parked car we'd struck), but the experience was nerve-racking from start to finish. For days afterward, I'd waited for a knock at the door—for Sheriff Keller to
appear, looking grim or embarrassed, telling me the jig was up.
But the visit never came.

Weeks went by, the real mugger was caught, and the sheriff's office made a formal apology to Malcolm and his grandmother for the way the case had been handled. The switchblade
had never been noticed missing. When the deputies searched
the station house after I got away, of course they found nothing
suspicious. It never occurred to them that I could've been
returning something, rather than taking it.

Veronica's story was never challenged, Jughead and Toni
were never questioned about the stolen car, Huxley told no
one that he'd even seen Kevin that night, and Cheryl and I
parted ways after our wild ride with only a single witness—the
old woman with her dog—to our escape. And as far as I knew,
she'd reported nothing of use to the sheriff.

So how had Poison Pen figured us out?

I tried to put together what clues I could . . . but I had none.
In fact, I didn't even know what kind of photos Archie was
talking about—only that they must be truly incendiary, or
Veronica would never have exposed Senator Pendergast. Not

after the speech she gave me at the library—*"I am done being messed with!"* And Archie believed the threats seriously enough that he didn't even dare send me a text with a warning, but instead stashed his communications inside a Trojan horse.

Burying my face in my hands, I bent forward, heart racing so fast I felt sick. *"How do you suppose the admissions board at Yale would react if they learned how smart you really are, Betts?"* I'd pushed myself to the absolute limit, carving out a new future after the one I'd planned for was destroyed by the taint of Hal Cooper's name. But Archie had needed help, and I was determined to ride to the rescue one last time.

When he told me he'd stolen that knife, I'd flipped out. On an impulse, trying to do the right thing, he'd made an error in judgment that stood to condemn him and Malcolm both. When a crucial piece of evidence went missing for a case in which Archie had already made himself a nuisance, neither Tom Keller nor Deputy Huxley would have to think back very far to remember when and where the switchblade had last been seen. To remember they'd left it in a room, unattended, with a friend of the suspect.

Given the audit, Sheriff Keller would have risked his job (again) if he didn't come down hard when the theft was exposed. Mrs. Andrews had been acting as Malcolm's lawyer, and Archie had been his self-appointed advocate . . . and that one simple, unthinking act—no matter how well-intentioned—could have ruined all three of them.

Someone had to do something, and so of course I decided it had to be me. And the worst part of it all? The only person I was trying to prove my worth to was *myself*.

"You've had such a hard time living down your father's reputation— how hard will it be to live down your own?"

I didn't know. But with no clues to work from, multiple lives hanging in the balance, and Poison Pen's deadline approaching at breakneck speed, I was going to find out.

Hands shaking, I opened my laptop and started typing out my confession.

CHAPTER TWENTY-FIVE

Once upon a time, my mother had a master key to the offices of the *Riverdale Register*. I could have kicked myself for not thinking to have a copy made for my own use. Not because I should have foreseen something like this coming (although, let's be honest . . . in Riverdale? Maybe I should have), but because the paper's archives contained a boundless wealth of information. Over the years, we'd gotten into more than one scrape where this kind of local history gold mine would have been indispensable.

But I was fresh out of master keys. And so that night, dressed in black and armed with my trusty bobby pins, I prepared to commit my second B and E of the summer to help keep people I cared about from having their lives and futures destroyed.

Some of the people I cared about.

My fingers were unsteady as I worked the tumblers in the lock, crouched low and unnerved by every passing car. Writing out the story I was supposed to plant in the *Register*'s Friday edition had been agonizing, and I'd stopped at least two dozen times.

There was no way I could confess what I'd done without at least implicating Archie, and probably Kevin as well, but how could I write an article that threw any one of my friends to the wolves in my place? I'd finally just had to make a choice and hope the guilt didn't sink me forever.

When the lock finally yielded to my makeshift picks, I crept inside, keeping the lights off. A flash drive burned a hole in my pocket, bursting with incriminating words, but before I gave in, before I doomed us all on the front page, I had to make one last effort at figuring out who had us dancing at the end of their string.

Whoever had proof of our actions the night of July Fourth, they'd waited a while to spring their trap. Therefore, it stood to reason either that *this particular week* was somehow crucial to the execution of their plans, or that it had taken them more than a month to accrue their evidence.

In the case of the former, I had to take stock of what was special about the second week in August. One factor: Those of us who were going away to school would be leaving soon—if we were to be targeted in a revenge scenario, it was now or never. Another factor (and the one that made my mouth water) was the Pendergast connection.

All this kicked off with Pernilla's engagement party, where the senator's affair was made public. Even people who reviled politics could be touched by human-interest stories of love and family, but one of the biggest and easiest PR moments of

Pendergast's campaign had turned into an utter nightmare, shaking his poll numbers to the ground.

I didn't think the timing was a coincidence.

As to the second possibility . . . well, that was also suggestive. If someone had taken a month to investigate the break-in at the station house, to figure out who was behind it and how it was worked, that told me a few things. First: This was personal (already established). Second: Poison Pen had serious resources, which likely meant money. And third: Something—or someone—had pointed "PP" in the right direction to look.

It was, I supposed, possible that all assumptions were true: Poison Pen had needed time to track down proof, but the decision to execute the scheme now—this week of all weeks—was also significant.

What I was hoping was that something in the *Register*'s coverage, whether about Pendergast or the Loomis mugging or the events of July Fourth, might give me a desperately needed clue. The car theft in Greendale, Veronica's vandalism report, and the "shots fired" outside the station house had all rated mentions in the local news.

But the authorities had buried any mention of the actual break-in. They'd never even been sure a crime had been committed at all. But Huxley firing live ammo at a civilian for no good reason was another black mark against the sheriff's office. So the deputy had concocted a story about a reckless driver trying to run him down while he was on a cigarette break, and how he'd tried to shoot out their tires.

It was a ridiculous explanation—but then, this was Riverdale.

With precious little time and nothing to go on, I delved into the *Register*'s archives. I intended to work forward through time, beginning with the July 5 edition and continuing to the present, figuring I could take until the last possible second to do my research.

And, somehow, I struck gold on my first try.

The headline story for July 5 was the fireworks spectacular in Pickens Park, with the Greendale car theft buried deep and the parking garage vandalism appearing only on the police blotter. There were scattered mentions of Senator Pendergast and his campaign . . . but on page two, a more harrowing story caught my eye.

HOME INVASION LEAVES LOCAL WOMAN IN CRITICAL CONDITION

The article was short, only a scant few paragraphs, but by the time I reached the end of it, all the blood had drained from my face. I read it a second time, and then a third, piecing everything together—and finally, I understood. Except for one detail, I had it figured out.

I know who Poison Pen is.

Veronica:

B, whatever you're thinking—don't. I was sure I knew who PP was, too, and I almost ended up in the morgue! This lunatic has eyes in the back of their head, and for all we know, they're reading our texts right now!

Betty:

That's . . . actually possible? But if I'm right, it's worth the risk. I'm pretty sure I can stop this before anyone else gets hurt.

Veronica:

"Pretty sure"?

Betty:

I've got a plan, but I'm going to need help— from everyone who was involved on the fourth.

Veronica:

I already regret saying this, but . . . okay. If Betty Cooper says she has a plan, I know it's one I can trust. Just tell me what I need to do.

CHAPTER TWENTY-SIX

The chance I was taking was a big one, much bigger than I even cared to admit to myself as I parked my car on the shoulder of a lonely road that ran alongside Sweetwater River. It was late, the moon casting silvery light through a mist that rose from the water's turbulent surface. The master file of the *Register*'s morning edition had already been transmitted to the printer—without my grand confession—so if this gambit didn't pan out . . . well, at least I could stop worrying about making a good impression at Yale come the fall.

Gravel crunched underfoot as I made my way to the bridge over the river, its boards lit a garish amber by sodium-vapor bulbs. The maples were as dense as an army where they crowded the verge, and I felt conspicuous—vulnerable. An owl hooted in the trees, and even this late at night, the air was sticky with residual warmth. Looking around, hands clenched into tight fists, I shuddered.

Despite an important question I still couldn't quite answer, I knew my theory was right. I was sure of it. When I texted the person I suspected of being Poison Pen and asked them to meet me at the Wesley Road Bridge . . . they hadn't asked *why*, they'd asked *when*.

Tonight, this was all going to end.

I just had to hope that I was better at bluffing than they were.

Approaching headlights cut lines through the billowing mist, and I stepped instinctively back into the gloom. A battered hatchback screeched up behind my own car and came to a sudden, rocking halt. The engine cut off, the door opened, and a shadowy figure emerged. Stalking forward, shoulders raised defensively, the newcomer stopped short just as the glow of the sodium lamps revealed a familiar face.

"All right, Betty," Ethel Muggs snapped from the dim golden penumbra. "Why am I out here in the middle of the night?"

Her eyes tracked me as I emerged from the darkness, and it took me a moment to find my voice. "I think we both know the answer to that."

"Really?" She sounded . . . amused? Disdainful? In the half-light, her eyes were flat and blank. "Sorry, but I've got no clue what you're talking about. You'll have to fill me in."

"Fine." I took another step forward, the old boards of the bridge creaking under my feet. "You're Poison Pen."

Ethel didn't react right away. For a moment, she just stood very still—and then she joined me on the bridge. Mist drifted between us, a tawny cloud clinging to our exposed flesh. "Is that supposed to mean something to me? 'Poison Pen'?"

"On the night of July Fourth, two men broke into your house," I said softly, the details of the story from the *Register* seared into my memory. When I'd seen the name Muggs in print, it had set all my alarm bells ringing. "You'd gone to Pickens Park for the fireworks show—along with most of the town—but your mother had a migraine, so she turned out all the lights and stayed home. Alone."

Ethel didn't even flinch. She might as well have been a wax dummy. "So?"

"So, on a night that they knew most of Riverdale—including almost every single deputy—would all be in one place, two burglars went looking for an empty house to rob. And they chose yours."

Ethel's eye twitched. "Yes."

"They thought there was no one home, because all the lights were out. And there was a window on the ground floor that was cracked open to let in the night air." This detail had been in the article I'd read. "That's how they gained access to the living room."

"We left the window open because our air conditioner broke down in June, and we hadn't been able to replace it yet," Ethel stated, expressionless. "We still haven't. Every store in town has been sold out since this heat wave started."

I swallowed. "When your mother heard the intruders, she called for help . . . but there was no answer."

"No." Ethel's voice was cold enough to freeze the

Sweetwater. "There wasn't. Because *for some reason*, the station house was completely empty when my mom was in the middle of an emergency. The phone just rang and rang, and no one answered."

I swallowed again. Vivid in my memory was the sound of a telephone, jingling away at the front desk as I was getting ready to break into the evidence locker that night. "So your mother tried to escape—"

"*No.*" Ethel stopped me, her voice sharp enough to cut through steel. "When no one answered at the station, my mother called *me*. I was at Pickens Park, and my mother called, begging me for help—begging me to *save her*. But I couldn't. And do you know why?"

Ethel took another step forward, her eyes glittering when the light caught them, and I shrank back against the railing. Below me, the river rushed and burbled around a fleet of heavy boulders—each one big enough and sharp enough to break any bones that mattered.

Her face dark with fury, Ethel demanded again, *"Do you want to know why, Betty?"*

CHAPTER TWENTY-SEVEN

ETHEL

If you'd asked me what I loved most about Riverdale, I doubt Pickens Park would even have rated in my top five, and yet, the night of July Fourth, it felt like the bare essence of everything I wanted to remember about my hometown. Music and laughter, shared memories and shared happiness. It was good, wholesome fun at its best. No murder, no suffering, no cults or killers—just a community coming together after so many hard years.

I'd claimed a spot on the grass, with a can of soda and a picnic dinner, and I was watching rockets burst in the sky.

And that's when my phone rang.

"Ethel!" It was my mother, her frantic whispering strangled by tears. "Baby . . . there's someone in the house!"

"Mom?" I jerked upright. Suddenly, the music and laughter wasn't so fun anymore. I could barely hear my mother's panicked whimpering. "What are you talking about? What's going on?"

"There's someone in the house!" she repeated sharply. "I can hear them downstairs! I called the cops, but no one answered, and . . . and I don't know what to do!"

Jumping to my feet, the park swaying around me, I barked,

"You have to get out of there! Go to one of the neighbors!"

"You don't understand," she moaned, and the sound was a knife in my chest. "My head . . . just trying to speak makes me feel like I'm going to vomit."

"Mom . . ." But I didn't know what to tell her. "Keep calling the sheriff. Just . . . keep calling! And try to make it down the back stairs—please, Mom, promise me you'll try!" I was already running, weaving between all the half-drunk idiots who littered the grass in the park. "I'm on my way, all right? I'll be there as soon as I can!"

"No! Don't come home, Ethel," my mom pleaded, her voice breaking, and tears streamed down my cheeks. "I don't . . . I don't want you to get hurt—"

"Mom, hang up the phone and try the police again!" I commanded, ending the call before she could hear me break down.

The world dissolved behind a blurry curtain of tears as I raced along the sidewalk, sprinting five blocks and taking a corner near the sheriff's office itself. I'd parked as close to Pickens Park as I could—but with so many people gathering for the festivities, the only free spots to be found were still incredibly far away.

I was out of breath and gasping for air as I finally reached the place where I'd left my car . . . and I came to a staggering, incredulous halt. There it was, sitting at the curb—but it was destroyed. It had clearly been struck by another vehicle going unbelievably fast, the bumper ripped free and one of the front wheel wells completely caved in. The door was crumpled, the side mirror missing, and the tire had been separated from the axle.

Panic made my vision sparkle, and a high-pitched noise came from the back of my throat. The door was so damaged I couldn't even wrench it open—and even if I could've, there was no way I could drive it on just three wheels.

This can't be happening.

"Is this your car, dear?"

I whirled, my heart thundering, rage and fear and confusion muddling my thoughts. An old woman stood on the sidewalk, holding a little dog on a leash. Mutely, unable to speak, I jerked a nod in response.

"I saw it happen." Her voice was heavy with sympathy. "The driver came out of nowhere, from that direction"—she pointed—"and nearly ran over me and Mopsy as we were crossing the street. They didn't even slow down! It's shameful, what's happening to this community. Riverdale used to be a nice town."

"They just . . . they just drove off?" Outraged and on the verge of tears, I could feel my hope slipping away—something cold and ugly stealing into my heart instead.

"I didn't think fast enough to look at the license plate," she told me apologetically. "I'm sorry. But I did catch a glimpse of the girl behind the wheel. She had red hair and bloodred lips, and she was wearing gloves. Struck me as odd, since it's been such a warm summer . . ."

"A girl . . . with red hair . . ." I repeated the words like an oath, like a spell, as if it might make the driver appear before me—so I could choke her until she was suffering as much as I was.

If she'd gotten out of the house safely, my mother would have already called me by then, I knew. But I checked my phone, anyway, and the screen was blank.

CHAPTER TWENTY-EIGHT

BETTY

"When I finally made it all the way back to my house, I found my mother at the foot of the stairs, bleeding from the head." Ethel's face was scarlet with fury, her hands clenching spasmodically into fists. "She had a skull fracture, a broken hip, and she'd shattered her left leg!"

"I . . . I read about that in the paper." My voice was unnaturally high. The railing of the bridge dug into my back, and I took a little step to the side—but there was nowhere to go. I'd chosen this isolated spot on purpose, because if Ethel and I were going to have a confrontation where crimes were confessed out loud, it had to be somewhere we wouldn't risk any witnesses; but maybe I wasn't nearly as smart as people said I was.

Eyes smoldering with rage, Ethel now stood between me and my car—and to my other side was nothing but the long, half-lit stretch of the bridge, extending into the darkness of Greendale. I might be able to outrun Ethel, but even if I could, where was I supposed to go?

"Oh, you did?" A smile twisted her face, sharp as a dagger,

and it was scarier than anything I'd seen yet. "Because I didn't exactly receive what you might call an *outpouring of support from the community*."

"Ethel," I began, my hands out between us. "You have to know how sorry I am about what happened to your mother. There was no—"

"'*Sorry*' is a very easy word to say, Betty Cooper!" Ethel growled the words with so much emphasis, spittle flew from her lips. "*Sorry* I wrecked your car, *sorry* I kissed your fiancé, *sorry* my dad killed a bunch of your friends!" Shaking her head violently, she went on, "But the thing is, it doesn't make any difference, does it? Because what's 'sorry' worth if there's no follow-through? Who cares how bad you feel about the stuff you've done if you *just keep doing it*? When Archie's dad died, we had an actual parade, but when Hiram Lodge drove *my* dad to attempt suicide, all I got was a handful of some sad dumpster flowers!"

"It was unfair," I acknowledged meekly. Ethel had moved closer, and I was more aware than ever of the turbulent water crashing around the rocks below—of the fragile railing that dug into the small of my back. "*This* was unfair. But what happened to your mom . . . none of us could have known. If we'd thought for a second that there was a ch—"

"But that's just it!" Ethel shouted. "None of you ever *think*— not about anything but yourselves! And for years, I've had to live in your shadows. We *all* have." Tossing her arms out, she exclaimed, "You've initiated gang wars and provoked serial killers, you've attacked people and started shoot-outs . . . but while you always come out on top, the collateral damage just piles up! Me, Midge, Dilton, my mom—it never stops!"

For a moment, I struggled to come up with a reply. Ethel appeared to be only a half second away from wrapping her hands around my neck—and, worst of all, she sort of had a point. In Riverdale, trouble came looking for you, rather than the other way around . . . but how many times had we made our trouble worse? My mouth dry, I stammered, "W-we never wanted anyone to get hurt that night. We were just trying to do a good deed."

"Oh, I know *exactly* what you were trying to do." Ethel's voice dripped with contempt. "How do you think I figured out who was behind it in the first place?"

CHAPTER TWENTY-NINE

ETHEL

June 23 was a busy night. After getting off work in the evening, I still had chores to do at home and a batch of cookies to bake so I had something to share at the community center's midsummer fundraiser. Okay, so I hadn't been personally invited, but it was open to everyone—and even if I wasn't really a part of Archie Andrews's friend group, I did admire what he was doing there.

With high school officially over, and all our lives diverging, it felt like an opportunity to make a gesture. Chuck Clayton, my dad, Dilton and Ben, the Sisters of Quiet Mercy . . . I'd endured a lot living in Riverdale, and I'd finally decided that I wanted to let go of the pain. I could never start over if I was always weighed down by a heavy past.

Good things had happened to me, too, don't get me wrong. My life wasn't all angst. But there were a lot of people in Riverdale that I was more than ready to leave behind—and not just the bullies on the football team. Whether it was because of something they'd done or because of who they were, I didn't have many good feelings attached to anyone bearing the names Andrews, Cooper, Lodge, Keller, Blossom, or Jones.

Was that unfair of me? Maybe. But I was ready to stop flinching whenever I saw one of those kids coming. To stop thinking about all the ways my life might be better if not for Hiram Lodge, Penelope Blossom, Hal Cooper, the Serpents, Ghoulies, and Gargoyles—and everyone associated with them. A peace offering of baked goods seemed like an appropriate farewell.

It was late when I left my house, the cookies still warm and fragrant on the covered dish beside me. But when I reached the community center, even though the lights were still on, Sketch Alley was silent as a tomb. My heart was sinking, even as I scooped up the cookies and hurried for the front door, sure I'd missed everything.

"H-hello?" I called out. The air conditioner whirred, echoing in the cavernous front room—but beneath the rumble, I heard voices. Hushed but intense, like when my parents would fight in their bedroom about my dad's business entanglements with Hiram Lodge.

Irresistibly curious, I drew closer to the source of the argument— the office at the back, the door of which sat just slightly ajar. Halfway there, I finally recognized who was speaking.

"You cannot be serious, Archie," Betty Cooper exclaimed, her voice rough and full of shock. "You stole evidence from the sheriff?"

"No! I'm telling you, it's not evidence." Archie was adamant. "Malcolm didn't do this! I don't care if the knife belonged to him or not, he's not the one who mugged that Loomis guy—whoever he is! You don't know him, Betty. He's a good kid."

"I *do* know him," Betty answered flatly. "And I actually happen to agree with you—but that's not the point."

"It *is* the point!"

"It's *not!*" There came a sound like hands slapping against thighs. "Archie, what good is it going to do for Malcolm when the sheriff discovers that the knife is missing and remembers that they left the box alone in a room with you? How does it help him—or Munroe, or their grandmother, or *you*—if you get busted for tampering with evidence?"

"The Moores don't deserve what will happen to them if the sheriff's office presses charges against Malcolm." Archie's voice was low and serious. "And they'll do it. They're getting slammed in the press because of everything that's happened here, because that senator is trying to prove what a crime-buster he is! Sheriff Keller told me himself that his hands are basically tied."

"Archie, I don't know how to tell you this, but they don't need the knife to make their case anymore." Betty was urgent, distressed, and I inched closer to the partially open door. "It was seen by first responders, it was collected and photographed, it was printed, identified by the chief suspect . . . they already have enough documentation to prove every damning thing they'd need to prove! Even if losing track of it makes them look a little incompetent, when they find *your prints* on the evidence box, it's going to make things a hundred times worse!" She was out of breath by the time she was finished ranting. "You have a record, remember? And according to the *Register*, Laurence Loomis was a volunteer for Senator Pendergast's election campaign! They're going to throw the book as hard as they can at whoever did this, and considering you're an adult now . . . if they press charges against you, you can kiss your future good-bye."

There was a dreadful silence, the air ringing with it under the whir of the air conditioner's fan. Finally, Archie croaked, "I didn't think about that. I wasn't thinking about anything, I just—"

"I know," Betty cut him off. "You wanted to do a good thing for someone who's had a lot of bad things happen to him."

"He's innocent, Betty."

"I know," she repeated. "But this makes it look like you think he's guilty."

Silence. Then: "What am I gonna do?"

"Give it to me."

"No, Betty, I can't—"

"You can. You have to." Through the crack in the door, I saw her hold her hand out. "I'll think of something, some way to fix this. Maybe we can even get it back where it belongs."

"Is that . . . is that even possible?" Archie's voice was faint.

"No, but we've pulled off the impossible more than once, right?" Betty countered. Her hand was still out, still expectant. "We can do it again."

"Okay." There was another stretch of silence, and then a second hand reached out—Archie's—and I saw them exchange a clear plastic bag with a switchblade inside. "Okay. Thanks, Betty. You just . . . you don't—"

"Don't say anything else, Archie. Don't say anything to anyone."

Spinning on my heel, I scampered for the community center's exit, the cookies scenting the air in my wake—like a trail of incriminating bread crumbs.

〜〜〜

I spent the entire day of July 5 in my mother's hospital room, waiting for her to wake up—thinking about the reckless, redheaded driver who destroyed my car. Thinking about the fact that, when my mom needed help the most, she'd been left on her own. I'd had to call for a rideshare while standing by my wrecked car, and by the time I reached my house I was already far too late.

There was nothing to do in the hospital but play with my phone, watch bad TV on a washed-out set, or read the news. I did the first two until I was bored to tears, and then I finally picked up the *Register*. Beneath effusive accounts about the fireworks show I'd abandoned was a story about a deputy firing his weapon on a reckless driver—the vehicle in question matching the same description I'd gotten from the old woman with the dog.

On page two was the nightmarish story of my mother's accident. Two hooligans, out to fund their Fizzle Rock habit, broke in expecting the house to be empty. Attempting to escape, my mother—incapacitated by her migraine—encountered them at the top of the stairs. They were both arrested mere hours later at a bar in Greendale called the Devil's Bargain.

And then I reached the police blotter. There, amid all the reports of public intoxication and disturbance of the peace at Pickens Park . . . was one for vandalism—logged mere minutes before my mother called me, begging for help.

At 9:42 p.m. on July 4, two deputies were dispatched to Evelyn Street Park 'N Go on a claim of vandalism. A late-model Rolls-Royce was found damaged and defaced, with potential inference of a threat, on the second floor of the garage. The vehicle in question belonged to Mayor Hiram Lodge and was in use by his daughter. Deputies are investigating.

For a long time, I stared at the typewritten words, until I could read them on the backs of my lids when I closed my eyes.

∧∧∧

On July 6, the *Register* reported the discovery of a stolen car with extensive damage to its passenger side. Abandoned on a sleepy, residential street a half mile away from where my hatchback had been totaled, it was a de-registered coupe that had recently been sold to a scrapyard in Greendale.

Details were scant, but according to the brief article, it matched the description given by Deputy Hayes Huxley of a vehicle he claimed had almost hit him on the night of July Fourth.

It also matched the description I'd gotten of the car that crashed into mine and kept on going—the one driven by a red-head, on the same night and at the same time that Veronica Lodge had the only two available on-call deputies occupied. And my hands shook as I opened my laptop to access the message boards at Rumordale.com.

∧∧∧

MAINMUGGLE:

I HATE LIVING IN RIVERDALE!!!! This town is a pathetic joke, with a corrupt "mayor," whose whole family gets away with MURDER. It was actually a decent place to live before the Lodges moved here, and now it's just a freaking sewer full of liars and cheats and criminals who can do anything they want as long as a Lodge approves.

ROADRAGER:

I can't believe anyone was stupid enough to vote for Hiram Lodge for mayor. You ask me, Riverdale deserves what they get.

LILSTNICK:

I couldn't agree with you more, Mainmuggle. Every branch of the Lodge family tree is rotten to the core.

MAINMUGGLE:

No kidding. And it's time someone did some pruning, because they need to be taken down a peg.

LILSTNICK:

I guess you've met the family?

MAINMUGGLE:

Our paths have crossed too many times. I even made the mistake of thinking one of them was my friend once. Thank God I survived THAT temporary insanity.

LILSTNICK:

I'm sending you a DM . . . check your inbox.

CHAPTER THIRTY

BETTY

"Wait a minute, back up." I was so stunned that, for a moment, I forgot to be scared. "You got a direct message from *who*?"

"Someone who hates Veronica and all the rest of you even more than I do—if that's possible." Ethel's smile was wide and demented. "Nick St. Clair."

"Nick St. Clair," I repeated, my mind whirling as that missing piece slotted itself into the puzzle. A regrettably familiar character, Nick had been Veronica's frenemy back in her Manhattan socialite days, but since then, he'd evolved into a unilaterally hateful creep. "You're working with Nick St. Clair? You're *both* Poison Pen?"

For a wildly fearful moment, I darted a look around, taking in the lonely road, the moonlit bend in the river, the thick trees swamped in shadow. I could possibly outrun Ethel, and maybe even take her in a fight if I had to, but if she had an accomplice . . .

"*That* petty little coward? You've got to be kidding me. He refused to even set foot in Riverdale himself—he's scared that Toni will release some kind of tickle video?" Ethel actually rolled her eyes. "Anyway, he doesn't have the imagination for something like this. 'Poison Pen' was all my idea and all my doing. Nick was . . . let's call him my 'silent partner.'"

"He gave you the money you needed to track down proof against us," I deduced, breathing just a little easier.

"*Ding ding ding!* There's the quiz show cheater we all know and love!" Ethel sarcastic-clapped for me. "He bankrolled me, yeah, but that's not all he did. It's really thanks to him that I connected what happened on July Fourth to that conversation I overheard between you and Archie at the community center. Well, Nick and his father."

I blinked, a connection swimming into place that I hadn't even considered. "Nick's father, Xander St. Clair, who happens to be—"

"Patrick Pendergast's chief opponent in the race for governor!" Ethel trilled, spreading her hands with delight. "Mr. St. Clair has had a private detective following Pendergast for months, digging up dirt on him and his family. That's how I got my hands on those pictures I made Veronica show everyone at Pernilla's engagement party. It's also how I knew Kevin was the one who made sure there was no one at the desk in the station house when my mother was calling for help, *afraid for her life*." Her face went dark again, her hands clenched tight. "It was pure coincidence the detective was out back that night, hoping to catch Deputy Huxley up to no good during a cigarette break. Nick didn't even know what the guy had caught on camera—he just had the entire album of photos sent over!

"When I recognized Cheryl behind the wheel of the stolen car, I finally started putting together what had happened." Dragging her fingers through her hair, Ethel paced a few steps to the left and then turned back again—still between me and my one real escape route. "Using Nick's money, I paid a hacker to access Riverdale's traffic cameras and confirmed that Veronica had staged her vandalism report. And I got Mr. St. Clair's detective to find the surveillance footage showing Toni and Jughead in Greendale that night, two blocks from the scrapyard." She spun around, eyes glinting. "And he already had pictures of you, Betty. You might as well have had your own name printed on that black hood you wore when you broke into the station house."

"So you pieced it together and decided to take us down." I was buying time now, trying to figure out how I could get around her . . . but I didn't see many options. "Was targeting Pendergast just a matter of convenience, or did Nick make that part of the assignment?"

"*I* was the one giving the assignments, *Betty*." Ethel's lip curled. "Nick did what *I* told him—not the other way around. Pendergast and Huxley made themselves into targets, and I used them because it got me what I really wanted. Understood?"

"Which was . . . ?"

"*TO MAKE YOU PAY!*" Ethel screeched, so loudly it made me jump, and I knocked against the railing with an unsettling *crack* of old wood. "It was time for you all to feel the way I did when my father almost died because of the Lodges! When my friends were killed by Penelope Blossom, and a role I deserved got handed to Cheryl on a silver platter! When my mother called me, begging for help, because the cops wouldn't answer her and she was *terrified*." She stomped closer, face glowing with rage, and I inched farther along the railing. "Do you have any idea what it's like to hear your mother sobbing and begging for help? How it *breaks you apart inside*?"

"Y-yes," I whispered. When the Shady Man was killed in our house, my mother had pleaded with me to help her hide the body. She'd been frantic, out of her mind with fear, and I'd done what she'd asked because a primal part of me could never have denied her—no matter how badly I wanted to. "But, Ethel, you can't do this—"

"Don't tell me what I can't do!" She grabbed me by the shoulders and slammed me against the railing. The wood splintered and gave, and I let out a shriek as I tipped backward, as I heard something splash into the roiling water below. "After everything you and your friends have gotten away with, *don't you dare* tell me what I can and can't do!"

"ETHEL, STOP!"

Those same words were on the tip of my frozen tongue . . . but it wasn't me who shouted them. Her fingers still hooked into my flesh like talons, Ethel shot a glance over her shoulder as Veronica Lodge leaped out of the shadows on one side of the bridge. She was followed closely by Archie and then Kevin—while from the woods on the opposite side of the narrow lane, Jughead, Cheryl, and Toni scrambled into view.

"Let her go, Ethel, please!" Archie implored from the foot of the bridge, holding out his hands. They all hovered, afraid to come closer—afraid to set her off. "Don't do something you can't take back, or you'll spend the rest of your life regretting it! Believe me, I know."

"All of us know what it means to screw up badly and try to fix it later," Jughead added, holding eye contact with her. "I stole that car because I wanted to help someone undo a mistake before it was too late."

"But there's no such thing as 'undoing.'" Kevin's voice was steady, even though his eyes were so wide they practically glowed in the moonlight. "There's only living with it. If you hurt Betty . . . you'll be no better than we are."

"In point of fact, you'll be worse!" Cheryl chimed in, and Toni elbowed her in the ribs.

"*Babe.* Not now."

"What are you talking about?" Ethel blinked, tense all the way up to the vein pulsing in her right temple. "I wasn't going to *hurt her.*" Stepping back, she dragged me away from the edge of the bridge, from the railing—which sagged and broke apart instantly without my body acting as its counterweight. I fell to my knees, gasping for air even as Ethel shouted, "I just wanted her to know what you all put me through! And what are you doing here, anyway—is this an *ambush*?"

"No, Ethel." Veronica stepped onto the bridge at last, her voice thick with emotion. "It's an apology. The seven of us only did what we did to protect people we cared about, but we made mistakes along the way. We got so caught up in our mission that we didn't consider potential repercussions. Your mother was an innocent victim . . . and so are you."

"Perhaps we oughtn't throw around the word 'innocent' quite so freely," Cheryl interjected, moving to Veronica's side, "but otherwise, Veronica speaks for us all. We weren't thinking of anyone but ourselves. I've suffered much in my life, and I wouldn't want another soul to endure even a tenth of it." Steeling herself, she continued, "I'm the one who hit your car. It's my fault you were unable to reach your mother in her time of need, so . . . so if you must punish anyone, let it be me."

"No!" Jughead pushed past Cheryl. "The car she was driving had a faulty transmission, and that's why the accident happened. But I'm the one who stole it in the first place, so I'm the one who should take the heat."

"If I hadn't pulled those deputies out of the station house on a fake report to begin with, they would have been there when Mrs. Muggs called." Veronica shouldered Jughead aside. "It's my family you've got the biggest ax to grind with, anyway."

"If Huxley had been at the desk like he was supposed to,

that wouldn't even have mattered." Kevin threw his own hat into the ring. "He could have contacted my dad and told him it was an emergency. I put the whole town at risk!"

"Look, this 'I am Spartacus' moment is fun, but I actually have a question." Toni walked right up to Ethel, who was still rooted in place, hands balled at her sides. "You sent letters to all these jokers, tortured them and put them through the wringer . . . but not me. Why? I was part of this, too, but you only used me to hurt Cheryl."

Ethel swallowed audibly, blinking, and a tear rolled down her cheek. In a squeaky voice, she said, "Because you donated to the PleaseFundMe for my mom's medical bills."

And with that, Ethel started to sob and fell upon Toni in an awkward embrace.

Veronica helped me to my feet, wiping away my tears, and gave me a worried look. "Are you okay, B? For a minute there, I was terrified that you were going to be sent on a swan dive into the Sweetwater."

"I'm okay." I nodded compulsively, trying to convince myself. "I really don't think Ethel intended to hurt me. She didn't know the railing was weak."

At least, that's what I chose to believe as I watched "Poison Pen" sob into Toni's shoulder. The truth was, whether she'd meant to harm me or not, Ethel could have—and she had a right to be furious with all of us. Archie made a misguided decision on the spur of the moment, sure . . . but I had spent a lot of time carefully planning out the rest of the bad decisions that followed.

"Ethel," I said, my voice still a bit shaky. "The reason I brought you out here is because we want to do whatever we can to help you and your mother. We can't undo what happened, but I can use my mom's connections at the *Register* and RIVW to get more attention for your PleaseFundMe. Maybe we can even get a follow-up story about your mom's recovery process, to encourage more people to give."

"And whatever donations you get, I'll match them." Veronica gestured. "If it's more than what I can personally afford, I'll pressure Daddy into covering it. It's the least he owes your family."

"And we're happy to move your mother into Thistlehouse until she's well enough to care for herself again," Cheryl pledged, watching her girlfriend closely in the event that Ethel's hug turned into an unexpected throttling. "Nana Rose has needed a physical therapist for a while, and we have one on retainer. She comes by several times a week, and it would be my pleasure to cover your mother's treatments."

"I can fix your car." Jughead rammed his fists into the pockets of his jeans. "It's not much, but . . . with the medical bills piling up, maybe it'll help with your expenses?"

"I can't do what everybody else can," Archie said with a faint smile, "but I know how to take a punch. So if you want to hit me, it's cool. I probably deserve it."

To my surprise, Ethel spun away from Toni and slammed a fist into Archie's jaw. He reeled a step, seeming more shocked than in pain, and then she collapsed against his chest, sobbing all over again—and he put his arms around her, holding her while she cried.

"Okay," Ethel finally managed, her voice thin and choked. "I don't know if I forgive you all, but . . . okay. I can't spend the rest of my life being this *angry*. If you really do what you promised, I'll . . . I'll let it go. I'll get rid of the evidence." Wiping her face, she said, "The St. Clairs haven't seen anything, so you don't have to worry about them. And Nick will never let Toni or Kevin be identified, because he's too scared of that video getting out."

Kevin and Toni exchanged a smug look—but then they joined Archie and Ethel's embrace. And then Cheryl did, and Juggie, and then Veronica and me. And as Sweetwater River crashed and burbled through the rocks below us, and my panicked sweat slowly dried in the waning heat of a long, terrible day, I realized that this was possibly my last intrigue in Riverdale for a while. Maybe for the rest of my life. A beautiful notion.

And if there was a more fitting way to say good-bye to the town I loved and loathed, I couldn't think of one.

So that's how it ends—not with a bang, but with a whimper. I'd call it pitiful . . . but then, it turns out that the one whimpering is me.

Let there be no misunderstandings: I'm not giving the "Core Four" and their trio of bumbling sidekicks a free pass. Just because no one is going directly to jail doesn't mean they're all passing Go and collecting two hundred dollars. But anger and resentment rot you from the inside out, and if you don't learn to let them go? Before long, you'll find out that <u>they</u> have hold of <u>you</u>.

Sooner or later, everyone's true nature wins out. When the pressure is on and the stakes are high, that's when your genuine self is revealed. The choice you make without thinking, the choice you <u>commit</u> to, consequences be damned? That's who you really are.

Even when you're standing at center stage, you'd better remember that every supporting player around you is the star of their own personal show. And you never, ever want to get in the way of another diva's spotlight.

The audience won't be the only ones watching.

—Poison Pen